CHRISTMAS CHOCOLATES AND CRIMES

A CHOCOLATE CENTERED COZY MYSTERY

CINDY BELL

ISBN-13: 978-1979828215

ISBN-10: 1979828210

CONTENTS

The small classroom was filled with eager students. Charlotte was a bit amused by the fact that it felt as if she was back in school after so many years. If the truth were told, she was never the best student, as her interests always ran along more creative lines. But she did enjoy the social aspect, which she was lucky enough to be enjoying again. She smiled at a few people with familiar faces, and even those that she didn't know, then focused her attention on the teacher at the front of the room.

"The key to making a good homemade Christmas gift, is to put equal parts thought and time into it. I've seen lots of these cutesy ideas on the internet, and sure they look great, but will people ever really use them? Will these crafts last past the season? We want to make gifts, not clutter. So, my focus here is to help you create gifts that are not only breathtaking, but useful, and long-lasting. Of course, edible gifts only last so long, especially if they're delicious."

The woman at the front of the classroom grinned at her own little joke. The other students, including Charlotte, obliged her with a smattering of laughter. She adored Beth, the woman who was running the class. She was soft-spoken, until the subject of crafting came up. Then her passion came out. She could chatter for hours about the pluses and minuses of different kinds of paint, or the best tools to use to create different projects. Thanks to her, the halls and windows of Freely Lakes were always tastefully and uniquely decorated. Charlotte was eager to speak with her privately, as she'd mentioned that she had a surprise for her.

"So, if you are giving edible gifts this year, the one thing I would recommend is to make the packaging part of your gift. Some people like to just wrap it up in a basket, or a plain box. But a tin, or a painted wooden box, is something that can last your loved ones a lifetime. I have some stencils here that you might want to try out." She gestured to an assortment of stencils spread out across the table.

"Some are holiday-themed, others are winter-themed, and some are just fun. Don't ever feel limited by the holiday, you don't have to make things holiday specific. Especially if you are creating something that you'd like the recipient to be able to use all year long."

As the other students approached the front table to retrieve stencils and wooden boxes, Beth waved Charlotte over to another table.

"I found something I thought you might like during one of my craft store shops. I'm sure you already have some, but I saw these, and I thought of you." She smiled as she presented her with a stack of plastic chocolate molds. "See, some of them are quite detailed, there's one with Santa and his sleigh. I thought with all of the Christmas orders you have at the chocolate shop, you might like these."

"Oh, I do!" Charlotte pressed her hands to her chest as she gazed at the molds. "They're just perfect. I've never seen anything like them. How much do I owe you for them?" She began to rummage in her purse.

"Nothing. They're a gift. 'Tis the season, right?" She met Charlotte's eyes. "Don't think I don't know that the only reason my class is filled to the brim is because of your recommendations. I can't thank you enough."

"Beth, it's full because everyone knows how great your classes are. Thanks for these. They are really going to come in handy." She carried the molds back to her table, which she shared with another woman, Diana.

"Aren't those just beautiful?" Diana gushed over the molds as her eyes sparkled behind her wire-rimmed glasses. "I've been trying to come up with just the right item to package in my giftboxes. I definitely want it to be candies made from these molds. Can I place an order with you now?"

"Sure." Charlotte smiled at her, but inwardly she wondered just how many pieces of chocolate she and her granddaughter, Ally could make before the season came to an end. The shop was already buzzing with customers throughout the day, and the orders kept rolling in over the phone. They were already stretched pretty thin, but she would never turn down a friend. In fact, she would never turn anyone down.

Ever since she moved into Freely Lakes, a retirement community nestled on the border of the pristine small town of Blue River and the slightly larger town of Freely, she'd made many new friends.

Even though she'd lived in Blue River her whole life, there were some people from Blue River and the surrounding towns that she hadn't had the chance to get to know well, and Diana was one of them. She hoped that their friendship would continue to grow.

As Charlotte began to decorate her own giftbox, she felt a small pang of guilt for being at the class, instead of at the shop with Ally. She'd opened the chocolate shop when Ally's mother was young and had run it alone, and now her granddaughter had taken over as manager. However, she still felt responsible for it, and she knew that Ally was working well into the night to keep up with the orders. But Ally had insisted that she attend the class. Ally was just as stubborn as she was, so there was no arguing.

"I've got my list of people that I'm giving gifts to." Diana sighed as a shadow crossed her features. "It's so hard to choose. I can't give everyone a gift, but I always feel like I'm leaving someone out. It makes me feel so guilty."

"Oh, you shouldn't feel guilty. You're such a giving person, and that spreads. Because you give to someone, that inspires them, and they give to someone else, see how that works?" Charlotte smiled and patted her shoulder. "Besides, the season isn't about who gets what, it's about all of us coming together as a community to celebrate, right?"

"Right." She smiled with relief. "Thanks, Charlotte, you've made me feel so much better. You are a dear soul." She took her hand and gave it a squeeze.

"So are you, Diana."

Charlotte smiled to herself as she sorted through the molds. It always made her feel good when she was able to cheer someone up. There was a time when she was the one who needed cheering up, after her daughter passed away, so she was happy to be able to return the favor to others.

As the class wrapped up for the night Charlotte gathered up her things. On the way out the door she waved to Beth, as well as Diana, then headed down the hall. One of the things she liked the most about Freely Lakes was all of the activities that were available right on the property. She could stroll home within two minutes from the classroom. It also meant she was always only seconds away from a friend. In particular, one special friend, Jeff. Lately, they'd been spending quite a bit of time together, and she'd even invited him to spend Christmas with her, Ally, and Luke. It made her a little nervous to care for someone so much, but she knew that Jeff was a trustworthy man. As she headed back to her apartment she placed a call to Ally to update her about the new order and see how things were going at the shop.

~

*A*lly poured the last of the melted chocolate into the molds, and blinked a few times to be sure that she could see clearly. Every muscle in her body ached. She was exhausted from arriving early, and staying late, just about every day that week. Making chocolate wasn't exactly a physically taxing job, but she'd barely had the chance to sit down, and making so much had certainly taken its toll. As much as she loved working in the chocolate shop, she longed for her soft comfortable bed. Still, the smell of chocolate soothed her, as it always had. Even as a little girl while helping her grandmother in the shop, the smell had been a healing balm for whatever ailed her. This evening was no different, as it distracted her from the soreness of her body.

It was fantastic that the shop was doing so well, but she had begun to consider hiring more help at least for this busy time of year. She was hesitant to, as her grandmother never needed to in the past, but

Ally felt as if she was relying too much on her help, when she was at a time in her life that she deserved more freedom.

After Ally set the molds to cool, she grabbed the broom to sweep up the front of the shop. A smile crossed her lips as she noticed the empty spaces on the shelves. The chocolate shop was decorated with wooden toys and ornaments, something that drew the attention of the young and the old. She rarely saw anyone come into the shop that didn't take the time to appreciate them. Around the holidays, the toys that were for sale would fly off the shelf, and along with them, some of Luke's wooden carvings. Her boyfriend had a special talent for whittling and had created some exquisite pieces. Of course, Ally always bought her favorite ones, though Luke didn't know that, otherwise he would insist on giving them to her for free.

Just as she thought of him, her cell phone began to ring. She smiled to herself as she saw his name flash across her phone. She never thought she'd be so giddy over a guy, but she was, even after all the time they'd spent together.

"Hi, did you land?"

"Yes, I'm here, but I wish I wasn't." He offered a drawn-out sigh. "I already miss you."

"Oh, you'll be fine." She laughed. "If I know you, you'll find an adventure before you even get checked into your room."

"It's not the same without you." He cleared his throat. "I could still buy a ticket for you to join me."

"You know that's impossible." She frowned as she traded the broom for a cloth to wipe down the counters. "This is the busiest time of year for us."

"I know, but that doesn't mean I can't dream, does it?" He chuckled. "It's only for a few days, but I am already counting them down. I'm looking forward to being back with you, in front of the fire."

"Mm, yes, me too." She smiled as she recalled the last evening they'd spent together. Her heart fluttered with the same desire that she could hear in his voice. "It won't be long, sweetie. We'll be back together in time for Christmas."

"If we don't get a blizzard." She heard the tension in his voice. "I warned the chief about the impending storms, but he still insisted I had to go to this convention. I think he just wanted me out of his hair."

"What hair?" She laughed. The current police chief was bald, in his mid-forties, and cranky. She had no idea how Luke put up with him. He barked when he talked, and didn't have any patience for

9

his officers. But Luke insisted he was good at his job.

"Good point." He laughed as well. "I'm sure you have a lot to do. I'll check in with you in the morning. Love you, Ally."

"Love you too, Luke. Try to have some fun, relax, and enjoy."

"I'll try," he grumbled, as if she'd asked him to complete the most difficult task. Luke was always a little intense himself, and it had taken a bit of a push on her part to bring him out of his shell.

After she hung up the phone she began to go through the routine of shutting down the register and taking inventory for the night. About halfway through the process her cell phone rang again. She saw that it was her grandmother so she picked up right away. Although there was quite an age difference between them, Ally still considered her to be her best friend, and she loved hearing from her.

"Hey, how did the class go?"

"You should see the chocolate molds that Beth gave me. They are just amazing! I can't wait to use them in the shop. I'm on my way home now. I just wanted to see how you were doing, and make sure you aren't working too late."

"I'm not, I promise, Mee-Maw. I'm closing up

now. There's something I've been meaning to talk to you about. What would you think if I hired someone to help out in the shop, just for the holidays? Someone that could be on the register, while we're making chocolates in the back, and can also help with the simple chocolate making if we have lots of orders."

"Uh, well, it's always been a family shop. But, since I have a new order for you from Diana, one of the students in the gift making class, I can't exactly advise against it." She laughed some. "Ally, you're the manager. I'll leave the hiring to you. Just be careful about who you hire, not everyone can be trusted."

"Thanks, Mee-Maw, I will be. I already have someone in mind. Nina, the woman I've been taking yoga classes with, is looking for some other part-time work. We've gotten to be quite good friends, and I think she would be a nice fit. What do you think?" She bit into her bottom lip as she considered it. She and Nina got along well while Ally was taking her classes, and she hoped they'd also do well together in the shop.

"I think that's a great idea. I don't know her though, so I can only go by what you've told me. She's fairly new to Freely, isn't she?"

"Yes, she moved there last year after her divorce. I'll see if she's interested. Thanks, Mee-Maw. Get home safe."

"I will. Good night, Ally. See you in the morning."

"Good night." Ally hung up the phone, then finished closing up. Maybe if she hired Nina, her grandmother would be able to take a few days off to rest and relax. She knew her grandmother hated being treated as if she couldn't do everything that Ally could do, but she worried about her working such long hours at her age.

After Ally locked up she walked to her car. She knew Arnold, her grandmother's pot-bellied pig, and Peaches, her cat, would be waiting at the door of the cottage for her. She was late with their dinner again, and they would both be quite upset about that. She laughed as she thought of all of the snorting that Arnold would do.

As always, Ally glanced back at the shop to be sure all of the lights were off and everything appeared to be in place. Satisfied, she climbed into her car. Before she started it, she sent a text to Nina to see if she would be interested in some part-time work at the shop. There was no point in putting it off any longer. If she wanted the extra help, this was the time when she needed it the most.

~

Charlotte tucked her phone back into her purse and continued down the hall. She knew she was nearing her apartment when she heard loud Christmas music. Her neighbor, Martin, didn't allow for the fact that their homes were indoors to stop him from decorating full force for the holidays. He framed his door with lights, as well as his inside windows that over-looked the courtyard. His walls on either side of his door were covered in flashing lights, and scat-tered around the entrance of his apartment were several moving Christmas figurines. To go with all of the decor, he had an assortment of Christmas music that played throughout the day and into the evening. Though it was a bit loud, he was within the regulations of the complex. Most of the time Charlotte found it cheerful and uplifting. On occa-sion, she would get annoyed by hearing the same song for the thousandth time, but that was usually when she was tired and generally a little irritable. The rest of the time she was grateful for having a neighbor who was into the Christmas spirit. Not everyone felt the same way, however. As she rounded the bend in the hallway she heard a raised voice, and the angry words that went with it.

"You turn it down right this second or I will call the police!" The voice belonged to another of her neighbors, Victoria. Victoria was quite rigid about the way she liked things, and ever since she'd moved in she'd given Martin and his wife a hard time about their decorations.

"You can't call the police, I have the right to play my music, I'm not breaking any laws." Martin's voice was just as loud, and his tone sounded a bit unhinged. Charlotte's stomach twisted. She doubted that the argument was going to fade any time soon. She was tempted to turn around and walk back down the hallway. It wasn't her business after all. But the only way to get to her apartment was past Martin's door, and she was exhausted from her long day. Still she paused, and hoped that the argument would stop within a few minutes. Instead, it seemed to get worse.

"I don't care what your rights are. I have the right to peace. I have the right to not be tortured by this constant drivel that you blast. No one wants to hear it, Martin. It's not even Christmas, yet! Can't you at least hold off until the day before?"

"Are you kidding me? Do you know how much I've invested in all of this? No, I can't just wait until Christmas. The point is to spread joy, and let me tell you, Victoria, you are the only one that is complaining. Everyone else always tells me how happy it makes them. So no, I'm not going to shut down everything just because you're a Grinch!"

"A Grinch?" Victoria shouted. "I'm a normal person who doesn't live in the darned North Pole. You're nuts if you think this doesn't bother anyone else, Martin. They're just all too polite to tell you. Turn it off!"

The pitch of her voice sent a shiver up along Charlotte's spine. She had the sense that things were about to turn physical. Without a second thought she hurried forward. She didn't want things to get out of control, and if there was anything she could do to stop it, she would. When the pair came into view, Victoria was nearly nose to nose with Martin, who was about three inches shorter.

"I'm not turning anything off," he growled as he glared right back at her. "If you don't like it, go live somewhere else!"

"It's not as if there is any other affordable

housing around here." She threw her hands up in the air. "Otherwise I would already be gone."

"Martin?" Trudy poked her head out through the door. In comparison to her blustering husband, she was a waif of a woman, with a voice to match. "Martin, please come inside."

"Can't you talk any sense into this buffoon?" Victoria locked her attention on Trudy.

"Don't you dare speak like that to my wife." Martin puffed out his chest and balled his hands into fists.

"Enough." Charlotte walked up to them, though her heart pounded. She didn't want Trudy to get tangled up in their argument. She always struck her as a sweet, but frail woman. "The two of you are acting like children, really."

"Who asked you?" Victoria cut her gaze sharply towards her.

"She started it." Martin shoved a meaty finger in Victoria's direction. "I was just enjoying myself, relaxing with my wife, when she came pounding on the door. Don't I have a right to my peace? Don't I?"

"Your peace?" Victoria nearly shrieked. "This is ridiculous, I'm calling the police right now." She pulled out her phone.

"And just what do you think the police are going to do about it?" Charlotte shook her head. She put her hands on her hips and tried to make herself as tall as she could. "Both of you drop it. You'll have this whole place in chaos if everyone sees flashing lights and hears sirens. Victoria, he has to turn the music off at ten, which he does every night. If you have a problem with it, I'm sure that you can find a nice brand of ear plugs to solve it. I know you are upset about it, but the police are not going to do anything about this, so you might as well just give up on that idea."

"Fine." She shoved her phone back into her purse. "If they won't do anything about it, maybe I will!" She swung her foot back and kicked a dancing snowman halfway across the hallway.

"Hey!" Martin shrieked. "That cost me money. You can't do that. Now, I'm calling the police! Get me the phone, Trudy."

"Now, Martin, please, do we really need to do that?" Trudy's voice shook as she questioned him.

"Oh yeah? You go ahead and call them!" Victoria spun on her heel and marched back to her apartment. She slammed the door so hard that the wall trembled.

"Get my phone, Trudy!" Martin shouted. Trudy

jumped at the harsh tone and trembled just like the wall.

"Settle down, Martin." Charlotte picked up the wiggling snowman. "She didn't do any damage. See?" She set it back into its place, and it began to dance as usual. "The police won't even bother to write up a report. It's best to just let all of this go. All right?" She met his eyes. "Just let it go."

"That's easy for you to say, you're not the one being harassed and threatened by that beast of a woman." He scowled as he looked over the snowman. "What kind of person beats up an innocent snowman?"

"The kind of person that's had enough of the Christmas music. I think you've done a great job here, Martin, but you could tone it down a bit, you know. The music doesn't have to be on all day, does it? Maybe if you agreed to certain hours with Victoria, all of this nonsense could be solved," Charlotte suggested.

"Never!" He narrowed his eyes. "I'll turn it up even louder. She's the one who started this war. We've been here for a long time, and there's no reason that we shouldn't be able to decorate the way we want to. And if you or Victoria have a problem with it, I don't really care."

"Martin. I never said I had a problem with it." Charlotte frowned, then looked past him at Trudy. "Are you all right, dear?"

"I'm fine." She nodded, then ducked back into the apartment.

"You should go inside too, Martin. There's no need to make more of this than you already have." Charlotte eyed him sternly. "It's the holidays, remember?"

"Right, whatever." He waved his hand, then stomped into the apartment after his wife.

By the time Charlotte reached her apartment, it was two minutes before ten. One minute later, the music turned off. Martin knew the rules, and he followed them precisely. She sighed as she settled into her favorite chair. If she wasn't exhausted from her day, she was definitely exhausted from the argument. She couldn't shake the memory of the way Victoria looked at Martin, as if she'd like to knock him out. She could only hope that it wouldn't escalate to that point.

CHAPTER 2

When Ally's alarm clock buzzed, she cringed and buried her head under her pillow. She didn't want to get up. Then she recalled setting up a meeting with Nina at the shop that day. That drew her out from under the blankets. Peaches opened one eye and gazed at her with annoyance.

"I know, I know, it's early." Ally stifled a yawn. "But, it's that time of year." She plodded her way into the bathroom, woke herself up with a shower, then tossed on some clothes. She was still bleary eyed when she turned on the coffee maker. She had just a few minutes to sit and wait for it to brew. As she nibbled on a muffin, her cell phone rang.

"Morning, Luke." She smiled as she answered.

"Good morning. Did you get any sleep last night?"

"Yes, I did. But not as much as I wanted." She laughed. "I think after New Year's, I'm going to sleep for a week. I've asked my friend Nina if she might want to help me in the shop part-time."

"Oh, that's great. Nina seems like a nice person. I've only met her a few times, but she's always so cheerful."

"She is. I think we'll do well working together. But you never know until you're in the situation, right?" She chewed on her bottom lip. "How is everything going there?"

"Cold. But otherwise good. I'm heading off for the first training session this morning. It should be interesting. It's all about the psychological perspective of a murderer. I tend to think people are a little too focused on that, but maybe the class will change my mind."

"Oh, that sounds like a great way to spend your morning. Very mind-stretching." She grinned. "Just think, you could be elbow deep in chocolate with me."

"Hmm." His voice trailed off as he stretched out the sound.

"What?"

"Oh sorry, I just got lost thinking about you covered in chocolate…"

"Luke!" Her cheeks grew hot even though he was several states away.

"What?" He laughed as he attempted to sound innocent. "You're the one that brought it up."

"Good point." She rolled her eyes and grinned. "Make sure you have a great day."

"I'm going to do my best, I hope you do the same."

"I will."

She hung up the phone and already felt pepped up even before she had her coffee. Luke always managed to fill her with enthusiasm and determination. After pouring herself a cup she took a few deep breaths of the steam. Her cell phone rang again. This time it was her grandmother.

"Good morning, Mee-Maw, how are you?"

"I'm okay." Her voice wavered some.

"Mee-Maw? What's up?" Ally narrowed her eyes.

"Oh nothing, just Martin and Victoria having their music wars again."

"Still?" Ally shook her head. "Victoria should give it up. Martin is never going to turn off that music."

"No, he's not." Charlotte laughed. "I'll see you at the shop in a bit?"

"Yes, thank you so much. I can't wait to see those molds you got. Oh also, I have Nina coming in to see how she likes things." Her heart fluttered nervously.

"Great, I can't wait to spend some time with her. Between the two of us we'll have her trained in no time."

"I hope so. See you soon, Mee-Maw." Ally hung up the phone and began to feel as if a burden had been lifted off her shoulders. She finished her coffee and was about to stand up, when Peaches jumped onto the middle of the table and gave a loud meow.

"All right, all right, breakfast is on its way!" Ally laughed as she hurried to get the cat's food ready. Arnold flicked his ears back and forth a few times, then opened his eyes. He was lying in the kitchen near the back door, ensuring that he never missed a meal. As soon as he heard the cat food can pop open he jumped to his feet and charged over to Ally. She reached down and rubbed the top of his head.

"Don't worry, Arnold, you're next."

Once she had them fed, she glanced at her watch. She was running a few minutes behind as usual. After a quick walk for Arnold, she kissed them both goodbye. Although they were pets, to her they were family. Her cat, Peaches was like a close friend. Arnold was her grandmother's pet, but she'd come to love him just as much as Peaches. With them in her home, she never felt lonely.

On the way to the shop, Blue River sprawled out around her. She loved her hometown, despite its limitations. It might take forever to get to a decent store, but the best part about the little country town was how close-knit the people were. She knew just about everyone, and just about everyone knew her. That could be a little daunting at times, but it could also be a great comfort. She parked at the shop while most of the others on the street were still closed. She headed to the front door and unlocked it. Right away she relaxed. Even though she had a ton of work to do, she still felt relieved to be in the familiar surroundings. It was her home away from home, and she was very grateful to be able to run it.

A few minutes after she arrived, Nina knocked on the front door. Ally opened it up for her and welcomed her inside.

"Hi there." She smiled. "I didn't expect you so early."

"Well, I figured if you were going to be here early we might as well be here together." She grinned, a charming grin, that made Ally certain that she knew some secret to happiness. Just behind her, Charlotte stepped inside.

"Good morning, ladies." She smiled at them both. "I brought the molds." She held up a bag. "Want to play with them, Ally?"

"I can't wait!" The three headed into the back. There was a window from the front of the shop into the kitchen. This allowed anyone who wanted to view the chocolates being made a peek into the process. Ally often forgot it was even there, but it did help add some natural light to the kitchen area.

As they worked together to create some chocolates with the new molds, Nina caught on quickly. Ally was impressed with how attentive she was. "Sometimes it can get a little boring because of how repetitive it can be," Ally offered in an apologetic tone.

"Oh, I don't think I could ever get bored with chocolate." Nina laughed.

"Help yourself to some samples before Mrs. Bing, Mrs. White, and Mrs. Cale get here." Charlotte offered her a tray filled with chocolates. "Those three are our best customers."

"When they pay." Ally laughed. "No, seriously,

they are in here every day at least once, and always keep us up to date with the local happenings."

"Yum." Nina plucked a dark cherry chocolate from the tray and popped it into her mouth. "Delicious. Are you sure you don't want me to pay you to work here?" She raised an eyebrow.

"Hmm, interesting idea." Ally eyed her with a light smile. "Or maybe we can just pay you in chocolate?"

"I'm not sure you'd have any left for the customers." Nina snatched another piece. "Is there anything that needs to be done before we open?"

"Just a few calls to make, and then a quick once over of the shop." Ally glanced up at the clock. "Oops, we've been chatting so much that we're running a little behind."

"You make the calls, I'll check over the shop." Nina picked up a broom. "Just in case." She winked.

"Thanks, Nina!"

Charlotte followed Ally into the back. "You were right, she's a keeper, Ally."

"I think so, too. We're going to have a great time working together." She picked up the phone from the desk. "I need to organize some pick-ups for today."

"I'll get started on the next batch of chocolates. Can you do me a favor and add Diana to your list of calls? Her chocolates should be ready in an hour."

"Sure, no problem." Ally began to call the number.

Charlotte made a few batches of chocolates, then stepped out into the front of the shop. Business was in full swing. Both Ally and Nina were behind the counter helping customers. Charlotte paused for just a moment to look at them. They were both so poised and friendly. Sometimes she wondered how so much time had passed. It seemed like yesterday that Ally held on to her knee for a ride around the shop. She pushed the thought away and stepped behind the counter to help them. After serving a few customers, Ally sent Nina for a break.

After another line of customers, Charlotte caught sight of a familiar face through the front window. She waved as the woman stepped inside.

"Hi, Charlotte." Diana smiled as she closed the door behind her. "I can't believe you have my order ready so fast! I'm so thankful."

"I knew you'd need to package them up so I wanted to make sure that you had them right away. Let me just get them from the back for you." She stepped through the door into the kitchen and grabbed a stack of three full boxes. When she returned, Ally was looking at pictures of Diana's painted boxes on her phone.

"Wow, these are beautiful, Diana." Ally handed her back the phone.

"Thank you. They are great for keeping bits and pieces in. I'm obviously not going to give you and your grandmother your own chocolates, but I can give you a giftbox if you want." She looked at the wooden items on display.

"Yes please! We can put it on display in the shop." Ally smiled. "You have real talent."

"Thank you, Ally, but you and your grand-mother are the talented ones. I can't wait to see how these turned out." She met Charlotte at the end of the counter.

"Here, take a look." She opened one of the boxes to show off the chocolates.

"Oh, Charlotte, they're perfect." She clasped her hands against her chest. "So darling, almost too darling to eat."

"Oh, but you have to try them." She gave her a piece of milk chocolate from the sample tray. "Never give away anything that you haven't tasted first." She winked at her.

"Thank you!" Diana squeaked happily and

popped the chocolate into her mouth. "Mm, mm, it melts in your mouth! So good." She sighed with pleasure. "What a perfect gift for Christmas. Everyone will be so happy to receive it."

"Yes, they will be, especially in that beautiful box. Are you going to need any help packaging them up?" Charlotte picked up one of the sample chocolates as well. It really was delicious.

"Oh no, I can do it. I hope to start delivering by this evening. Once I get them all handed out, then I can finally relax and enjoy my holiday." She sighed with a laugh. "It's a lot of work, isn't it?"

"Yes, it is." Charlotte grinned. "But well worth it." She rang the sale up on the cash register.

"Bye Ally!" Diana waved to her as she picked up her boxes of chocolates. "It was good to see you again."

"You too." Ally smiled as she waved back. "Enjoy your chocolates!"

The shop had no customers for the first time that day. As Ally turned to Charlotte to offer to make her a coffee, Beth came in the front door as Nina came in the back.

"Hi Beth." Charlotte smiled.

"Charlotte, when I walked past before it was so

busy I thought I would come back. Lucky I did, this is much better."

"Yes, we were very busy, but it's emptied out now." Charlotte smiled. "What can I get for you?"

"I wanted to pick up the chocolates and the chocolate covered Christmas tree cookies for my grandkids. Are they ready?"

"Yes, I'll just grab them for you." Ally smiled as she went into the kitchen. She returned shortly after with the boxes of chocolates and chocolate cookies and placed them on the counter. Ally opened the boxes for Beth to see.

"Oh perfect!" Beth smiled as she looked over the boxes. "I love the white chocolate on the cookies, it looks like snow."

"Try one." Ally handed her a spare cookie to try.

"Thank you." Beth bit into the cookie. "Mm, delicious."

"Mee-Maw, I'm going into the back to make another batch of chocolates. Nina is pretty good to go on the register if you want a break." She patted her grandmother's shoulder before she walked into the kitchen.

"Oh thanks, sweetie. Yes, we can use some more samples out here." Charlotte accepted Beth's payment. "Enjoy your chocolates!"

"I will, thank you!" Beth moved to pick up the boxes of chocolates.

"Here, let me get that for you." Nina reached for the boxes. "I can carry them out to your car for you." She offered a sunny smile.

"Why? Because I'm too old?" Beth eyed her with a frown. "I can carry candy, thank you very much." She picked up the four boxes, turned on her heel, and marched out of the shop. At the door she struggled for a moment to get it open, but managed to push through before either Charlotte or Nina could offer to help.

"Oh no." Nina shook her head as her eyes grew dark. "My first day, and I've already offended someone. I wasn't so sure I'd be good at the customer service part of this."

"You're doing fine." Charlotte met her eyes with a smile. "Beth is a very strong-willed woman, and you'll find out when you get to be our age that it can hurt your pride when a younger person offers to help with a simple task."

"I didn't really think about it. I suppose it was just instinctive to want to help." She rubbed her hands together and took a deep breath. "I'll have to remember to be more careful next time."

"It never hurts to offer to help a customer, but

you'll get to know them as they come in. Some people are friendlier than others, and some, like Beth, just want to be treated as an equal." She shrugged, then patted the counter. "You'll meet all kinds of people. That's one of my favorite parts of this job, you get the opportunity to get to know so many locals. There are very few people in Blue River and the surrounding towns that haven't passed through these doors at least once or twice. Trust me, you're doing very well. Don't let that little incident shake you up."

"Thanks, Charlotte." She grabbed a cloth. "I'll just wipe down the counters while it's not too busy."

Charlotte poured herself a cup of coffee before the next rush would come in. She was very impressed with Nina, and hoped that Beth's snide remark wouldn't scare her off.

The rest of the day went smoothly, though busy, and by the time four o'clock rolled around Charlotte was more than happy to let Ally and Nina close up.

"I want to show Nina the closing routine in case there's ever a time that she might need to do it." Ally looked over at Nina. "I wouldn't normally ask you to, but things do come up."

"Yes, they do." Nina shrugged. "I'm all ears."

"Great. Mee-Maw, you'll be okay getting home?" Ally looked into her eyes.

"Of course, Ally." Charlotte shot Nina a knowing look. Nina returned a sympathetic smile.

"What?" Ally looked between them with a bewildered smile.

"Nothing, sweetheart." Charlotte pecked her cheek, then headed out the door.

After Charlotte left the shop she decided to stop by Martin and Trudy's apartment. She wanted to do something to cheer them up after their run-in with Victoria the day before. Armed with a small box of chocolates she knocked on the door, and waited for someone to answer. The door swung open so forcefully that Charlotte took a step back.

"What do you want now?" Martin barked. His dark expression transformed when he recognized Charlotte. "Oh, Charlotte, I'm so sorry. I didn't realize it was you."

"It's all right." She cleared her throat as her heart still raced in reaction to his anger. "I should have called first."

"Please, forgive me. It's just that Victoria has already been over here twice today, and I assumed it was her again." His cheeks were flushed, whether from anger or embarrassment she couldn't be sure.

"I'm sorry to hear that, Martin. I brought you and Trudy something. Is she home?" She clutched the box of chocolates in her hands. If Martin was this angry, then how was Trudy holding up?

"No, she's not here." His voice grew rough again and he narrowed his eyes. "Thanks to Victoria we had a fight, and she left. I have no idea where she went, Charlotte. We've never had a fight like that before." His eyes moistened just before he closed them. "It's supposed to be Christmas, you know, this is the worst Christmas ever."

"I know. I'm sorry you're having so much difficulty. I'm sure Trudy just needed a break from all of the tension. She'll be back, Martin. All of this will settle down." She presented him with the box of chocolates. "This is for you. The two of you can share it when Trudy gets home. Try not to let all of this get to you. Victoria was wrong, most of your neighbors enjoy all of the hard work you put in. Don't let anyone tell you different. Okay?"

"Thanks, Charlotte." He sighed as he took the box of chocolates from her. "Diana is always talking about how delicious your chocolates are, and she is right."

"Then you're going to like your Christmas gift this year." Charlotte winked at him. After he closed

35

the door, she hoped that he would have a better evening. It worried her a little that Trudy had taken off. As far as she knew the pair rarely had marital problems, but then what happened behind closed doors in a relationship was not always public knowledge. As she headed for her apartment, her cell phone rang. She saw that it was Diana's number.

"Hello?"

"Hi, Charlotte, it's me, Diana."

"Hi, Diana, what's going on? You sound frazzled." Charlotte frowned as she unlocked her apartment door.

"I am frazzled. I thought I ordered enough chocolates but apparently, I didn't. I really want to get all of these gifts done tonight. Are you still at the shop? Is there any way that you could bring some home with you?"

"No, I'm not still at the shop." She stepped into her apartment and smiled at the familiar surroundings. "But Ally is, I can have her drop some by. How does that sound?"

"Oh really? I don't want to trouble you, but that would be so wonderful. You don't think Ally would mind?"

"No, she can drive past on her way home, I'm sure she won't mind. Let me just give her a call.

When she brings the chocolates I'll come right over, okay?"

"Okay, thanks so much! You're a lifesaver!"

Charlotte hung up the phone with a sensation of warmth in her heart. She was happy to help out a customer and friend, and Diana said such good things about the shop that she was owed special treatment. She placed a call to Ally and made the request. As she expected, Ally was happy to stop by.

CHAPTER 3

After such a busy day Ally was relieved to turn the lock on the front door. There was still work to do to close up, but at least she knew she wouldn't be battling another rush. She brushed her brown hair back from her face and tied it up in a tight ponytail. Closing up was less daunting with a companion to keep her company.

"Great job today, Nina." She smiled at her as she walked back over to the counter. Nina had already begun packing up the chocolates on display.

"Thanks, Ally, I really enjoyed it."

"Really?" Ally arched an eyebrow as she opened the cash register.

"Really. I have to admit, Ally, when you first told me about running the shop, I honestly thought it had to be the best job ever." Nina leaned back against the counter as she watched Ally finish shutting down the cash register.

"And now?" Ally pushed the drawer shut with her hip as she carried a pile of receipts to a file behind the counter.

"Now, I see that it's a great job, but it's also a lot of very hard work." She clucked her tongue. "You must be exhausted after a day like this."

"Well, it's not normally this busy." She filed the receipts then turned back to face her. "Normally we have a little more time to just chat with the customers. But during the holiday season it can certainly get a little crazy. Is it too much for you?" She met her eyes.

"No, I don't think so. I guess that's really up to you though. Isn't it?" She smiled, though it wavered some.

"Relax, Nina, I think you did a fantastic job. I'm really surprised that you picked everything up so fast. Not because I didn't think you could do it, but because I thought it would take someone a lot longer to get used to everything. So, if you're still interested, I'd love to hire you for the job."

"Absolutely." She clapped her hands. "I'm so excited."

"Great. I'm going to give you some paperwork to

take home. You can just bring it back with you tomorrow morning, then I can get the hiring process started." She thumbed through another file to find the right paperwork. From memory the shop had only ever employed delivery drivers and it had been so long since the shop had hired anyone that she felt as if she needed to blow the dust off the paperwork. "Oh, fair warning, there is a pen out back for Arnold, and on occasion my cat Peaches comes to work with me." She pulled the paperwork out and handed it to her. "Will that be a problem?"

"Only if you don't let me pet them!" She grinned as she took the paperwork. "I really can't thank you enough, Ally. Though, I should probably tell you, I upset your grandmother's friend, Beth today."

"You did?" Ally raised an eyebrow. "How?"

"I offered to carry her boxes of candy." She cringed.

"Oh, don't worry about that." She waved her hand. "You're going to get some people that can't be pleased. They'll be upset if you do offer, and just as upset if you don't. You did the right thing by trying to help her out. And thanks for reminding me, I need to grab another box of chocolates from the back to run over to my grandmother. Thanks for today, Nina, have a good evening."

"Thanks, you too." She hurried out the door towards the parking lot.

Ally looked up at the clock. It was nearly six. She had to get home to feed Peaches and Arnold, but then she would head back to the shop to finish a few more orders. After she ducked into the back to grab the box of chocolates, she took one more glance over the shop. Everything appeared to be in place. She locked the door behind her as she left. On the way home she stopped by Freely Lakes. She still found it a little strange to visit her grandmother instead of sharing with her the cottage she'd grown up in, but it was also nice for them both to have that space. It meant that she could look forward to visiting with her grandmother. As she pulled into Freely Lakes she smiled at the Christmas lights that lined the buildings. It looked a bit like a fairy tale castle the way it was lit up. She grabbed the box of chocolates from the passenger seat and carried it towards her grandmother's apartment. As she approached it, she heard loud Christmas music.

"I guess Martin is still at it," she mumbled. When she passed Martin's apartment she was stunned by the sight of Christmas figurines tossed all over the floor. She narrowed her eyes as she continued on to her grandmother's door. After a quick knock, Charlotte answered.

"Thanks so much, Ally. I'll run these over to Diana in just a bit. How was the rest of the day?"

"It was good." Ally smiled, though the expression faded quickly. "Have you seen the decorations in front of Martin's apartment? It looks like someone destroyed them."

"Oh no." She sighed. "I bet Victoria went after them. I'll go take a look. You get home and get some rest, okay?"

"Sure, I will." She kissed her grandmother's cheek. Of course, she had no intention of going home and staying at home, but she didn't need to tell Charlotte that. "Listen, try not to get too involved in things between Victoria and Martin, you know how these neighborly disputes can get out of hand sometimes."

"Yes. I do." Charlotte frowned. "Hopefully, it hasn't already gone too far."

Ally pursed her lips as she realized her grandmother had no intention of staying out of it.

Charlotte gave her granddaughter a quick hug, then released her so she could head home. She knew that she was only going to feed the animals, and then go straight back to the shop. Ally was determined to make every penny she could during the holiday season. Charlotte admired that about her, as she had always felt the same way. Valentine's Day, Mother's Day, and Christmas were big business boons for them, and their business relied on the extra money made from those special holidays to survive year round. After Ally left, Charlotte decided to check on the state of Martin's decorations. When she saw them, she felt terrible. She knocked on the door of the apartment. The door swung open so suddenly that she gasped.

"What do you want?" Martin barked at her. Anger twisted his expression, until he recognized her. "Oh, Charlotte, I'm sorry. I thought it was Victoria again." He looked past her at his decorations. "Oh no!" His voice raised again. "Did you do this? Why would you do this?" He practically screamed. Charlotte was so stunned by his anger that she barely noticed a few neighbors make their way past the scene.

"Of course, I didn't do this, Martin, I was just checking on you…"

"Get out of here! Get out of here now, Charlotte!" He grabbed some of the decorations only to throw them back to the floor. Charlotte's heart lurched. He seemed so angry, almost vicious.

"Please, Martin, is Trudy home, yet?"

"No, she's still not home. I think she's left me. She took off. All because of Victoria." He tore down the lights on one side of his door. She noticed that his face was covered in sweat.

"Martin, you have to calm down or someone is going to call the police!"

"Let them!" he shouted again, this time so close to Charlotte that she jumped back.

"Fine!" She turned on her heel and stomped away from his door. Once inside her apartment she took some time to calm down. She didn't want to spread her frustration to Diana, who she knew needed the chocolates. She placed a quick call to her.

"I have the box of chocolates, Diana. Would you like me to bring them now?"

"No, not straight away. I've already finished packing most of the boxes and I'm about to deliver some of them. You can bring it by after, is that okay?" She sounded so cheerful and relaxed. It was a relief after Martin's attitude.

"Okay, I'll come by in about an hour."

"Perfect. Thanks again, Charlotte." She hung up the phone.

Charlotte settled into her chair and closed her

eyes. She tried to forget about Martin's anger. Of course, he wasn't actually angry at her. She couldn't believe that Victoria would take things so far. An ill feeling brewed within her as she realized that their argument would probably lead to the police being involved, and maybe that was for the best. It didn't seem to her that either of them could control their tempers.

A little over an hour later, Charlotte headed for Diana's apartment. When she knocked on the door, there was no answer. Charlotte was surprised as she had let Diana know she would be stopping by. Was she still out delivering the gifts? She knocked again. Finally, the door opened.

"Hi!" Charlotte smiled as she held out the box of chocolates. "One more, just like you asked."

"Oh, thanks so much, Charlotte. Let me take those." She grabbed the box. Charlotte caught a glimpse of her living room and noticed boxes scattered all over her coffee table. She was surprised, as it looked like a mess and she thought Diana already delivered or at least boxed up most of the chocolates.

"Do you need any help, Diana?"

"No, I'm fine, thanks. Just a little busy. Bye now!" She waved as she pushed the door closed.

Charlotte guessed that she was embarrassed about being caught in a lie. She'd never point it out to the woman. It was clear to her that Diana liked to do things for herself, and if that meant she bragged a bit or made up some white lies, Charlotte didn't really mind. She walked back towards her apartment. She was a bit nervous to go by Martin's, but noticed that the decorations were back in place. Luckily, there was no sign of an argument, and her favorite Christmas song was playing. She started singing along to "Jingle Bells". That cheered her up a little.

Later that evening as Charlotte prepared to go to bed, she heard her favorite song again. She smiled, until she glanced at her watch. It was two minutes after ten. The music continued to play. Was it possible that Martin fell asleep and didn't realize what time it was? Why wasn't Victoria out in the hall hollering about the music? She stepped out of the apartment and glanced down the hall. No one else was in sight. She knew that if the music didn't turn off soon Martin could get in trouble, so she knocked on his door. After two sets of knocks with no answer, she touched the knob. It seemed odd to her to attempt to open someone's door, but her instincts told her that something wasn't right.

Neither Martin nor Trudy answered the door yet the music was still on? She pushed the door open, and saw the blood right away. It streaked the carpet and wrapping paper laying on the floor, and led to Martin's body. A scream escaped her lips as she realized that he was dead. In the hallway behind her Charlotte could hear voices, but she was too stunned to recognize them or understand what they said. It wasn't until the shrill siren of a police car broke through all of the noise that she realized someone had called the police. The next few minutes were a blur of police officers, and questions. At some point she managed to text Ally.

CHAPTER 4

*A*lly had just locked the door of the shop for the second time that night when she received a text from Charlotte. The message was a bit garbled, but what she could understand of it shocked her. Could Martin really be dead? She rushed to her car and drove straight to Freely Lakes. The parking lot was filled with police cars, and the flashing lights painted a garish blanket over the sparkling Christmas lights. She parked in the first place she could find and ran towards the door. As she reached it, an officer stopped her.

"Ma'am, are you a resident here?" He locked eyes with her.

"Petey, it's me Ally. I need to get in to see my grandmother." She started to push past him.

"I'm sorry, Ally, but I'm not supposed to let

anyone in or out." He pointed to the parking lot. "You can stay here if you want, but I can't let you through."

"Seriously?" She frowned as she studied him. "If Luke were here you would let me in."

"But he's not." He set his feet shoulder width apart and physically blocked the door. "Don't make this night harder, all right?"

The desire to argue with him was so strong that she had to bite into the tip of her tongue to prevent it. As much as she wanted to get to her grand-mother, she didn't want to do anything to cause problems for Luke.

"It's all right, Petey, it's all right." A firm hand clapped down on her shoulder, but it didn't feel reassuring. She looked over her shoulder to see the chief. "Come on in, Ally, I'd like to speak with you."

As he led her down the hallway that led towards her grandmother's apartment, Ally had no idea why he would want to speak to her. But she was relieved to be getting closer to her grandmother.

"Chief, what happened here?" Ally quickened her pace so that she was beside him instead of behind him.

"That's what I'm hoping you can get your grand-mother to tell me." He paused at the yellow police tape that surrounded Martin's apartment. Ally noticed the Christmas decorations, but someone had turned off the music, or maybe it was never on. Her head buzzed with confusion as the chief lifted the police tape and guided her under it. She saw little yellow markers on the carpet that designated where evidence of the crime still remained. By the time she spotted her grandmother on the couch with another officer beside her, she felt terrible.

"Mee-Maw!" She rushed over to her and threw her arms around her. "Are you okay?"

"Yes, I am." Charlotte looked at her and shook her head. "How could this happen?"

"Now, she can talk." The chief crossed his arms.

"Excuse me?" Ally shot him an impatient look. "She's obviously in shock."

"Clearly. But I still need to know what happened here." He locked his eyes on Charlotte. "Can you give me an idea of how this happened?"

"I don't know. The music was still on after ten, so I came over to check on Martin. When I knocked, he didn't answer," Charlotte fumbled over her words.

"And you just walked in?" The chief studied her intently. "You just thought it was okay to open the door?"

"You don't understand. Martin always turns the music off at exactly ten. It was after ten, and I thought maybe he'd fallen asleep or something. But when I knocked and he didn't answer, I was worried." She looked up at Ally with tears in her eyes. "Oh, Ally, who would do this to him?"

"That's what we're trying to find out." The chief narrowed his eyes.

"It's okay, Mee-Maw." Ally pulled her closer. "Let's get you home."

"No, she's not going anywhere." The chief moved in front of them both.

"What? Why not?" Ally frowned. "She told you what she knows. Why would you want to keep her here?"

"As of now, Charlotte is our only witness, and our only suspect. So, she's going to stay right here until I get a handle on what happened here."

"Suspect?" Ally stared at him, her mouth half-open. "Have you lost your mind?"

"Excuse me?" He took a step towards her. "Who exactly do you think you're speaking to?"

All at once Ally realized that this was no longer just a tragic situation, but a moment when her grandmother could be in quite a bit of trouble. She knew she needed to be far more careful about what she said.

"I'm sorry, you just surprised me. I can't imagine why you would ever consider her a suspect. However, if you're going to treat her as one, then maybe I need to call a lawyer." She folded her arms across her chest.

"Ally, it's okay." Charlotte patted her arm. "I'm willing to cooperate. I didn't do anything wrong. If it helps in some way to figure out what happened to Martin, then I am fine with it." She looked over at the chief. "I did not harm Martin. I don't know who did. When I came in, I saw him on the ground, and I screamed."

"Why didn't you call the police?" He pointed to her phone on the couch beside her.

"I was just so shocked, and then by the time I could think again, I could already hear the sirens. Someone had already called." She frowned. "It was clear that he was gone, it's not as if there was any chance of saving him."

"And how did you know that if you were so shocked?" His tone grated Ally's nerves.

"Mee-Maw, you don't have to answer any questions." Her stomach churned as she wished that

Luke was there. He would put the chief in his place even if it meant risking his job.

"You be quiet, or I'm going to make you wait outside." The harshness of the chief's gaze sent a shiver down Ally's spine. She had a feeling he was itching to see her in handcuffs. Why, she wasn't quite sure, but she didn't want to tempt him.

"All right, I apologize." She slipped her hand into her grandmother's.

"If you had nothing to do with this, then who do you think did? You live nearby, right? You know Martin and Trudy fairly well?" He crouched down in front of the couch so that he could look straight at Charlotte.

"Trudy!" Charlotte gasped and looked towards the bedroom. "Is she okay? Where is she?"

"That's what we would like to know. Do you have any idea where she might be?"

"Oh no." She clasped her hand over her mouth for a moment and tried to decide how much to share. She knew she needed to tell him everything, but it made her uneasy to share Martin and Trudy's personal business. "She must not have come home."

"What does that mean?" He straightened back up. "Anything you know that could help this investigation you need to tell me."

"Earlier, when I stopped in to check on Martin, because his decorations were all torn apart, he said that she left him. I just assumed she would be home by this evening, though." She wrung her hands. "They're normally a very happy couple."

"Hm." He nodded. "You said you stopped by earlier? I have a few witnesses who said they saw you and Martin arguing. Is that true?"

"Not exactly. He was angry, really upset because of the damage to his decorations. He did yell, but I think he was just frustrated with everything. He had the wrong impression that I might have destroyed his decorations."

"So, you didn't threaten him or tear down any of his decorations?" He kept his gaze steadily on her.

"No, of course not." She shook her head, then sighed. "I love the holidays. I liked his decorations."

"Look, I know you have a job to do, but my grandmother is exhausted. She's told you everything she knows. Can't you talk to her again in the morning?" Ally rubbed her grandmother's shoulder.

"Yes, all right." His expression softened some. "But be reachable."

"I will be." Charlotte assured him as she started to stand up. Ally took her hand and guided her out of the apartment.

~

*A*s Charlotte and Ally stepped out of Martin's apartment and into the hallway they were greeted by the curious gazes of several of Charlotte's neighbors. Charlotte noticed that Victoria wasn't one of them. Even though she could barely get two thoughts together, she considered it strange that Victoria, who lived right next door to Martin, hadn't poked her head out to see what was happening. She also noticed that her neighbors gazed at her with a strange look in their eyes. Ally opened Charlotte's apartment door for her and ushered her inside. Then she locked it behind her.

"The nerve of that man," Ally spit out her words. "If Luke wouldn't get in trouble for it, I would have told him exactly what I thought of the way he was treating you. I can't believe he even called you a suspect. What is he thinking?"

"He's just doing his job, Ally. You can't give him a hard time for that." Charlotte eased herself down into her chair. "He has to find out what happened."

"Yes, I know he does, but what I don't understand is why he would waste his time questioning you." She sat down on the couch across from her grandmother. "I mean, really. Does he think you went in there and killed Martin?"

"Ally." Charlotte grimaced.

"Oh, Mee-Maw, I'm sorry, that was insensitive. He was your friend. Are you okay?" She reached across and squeezed her grandmother's hand. "Can I get you some tea? Something to eat?"

"No, I'm okay, thank you."

"I can't believe this happened."

"Me neither. I was just going to bed." Charlotte shook her head slowly. "I was going to turn out the light and go to bed. But the music was still on, and I knew that wasn't right. So, I went to check. Maybe I shouldn't have opened the door. Maybe I should have just called the police."

"But what would you have told them? That your neighbor wasn't answering the door? I doubt anyone would have come out for that. Then when would someone have missed Martin? He was retired, and it looks like his wife left him, so how long might it have been before he was found?"

"Ugh, I don't even want to think about it." Charlotte sighed, then sat forward. "I think the only thing we can do, is try to figure out what happened. The chief is shorthanded with Luke and the other detectives away at that convention, so I doubt that he will be able to keep track of all of this himself. I think we should do our best to help." She met Ally's eyes with a look of determination.

"Okay, I agree." Even if Ally didn't agree she knew that she wouldn't be able to stop her grandmother.

"I just wish I had gone over there earlier. There must have been some kind of commotion. Why didn't I hear it?"

"The Christmas music." Ally shrugged. "It was very loud when I heard it earlier. I doubt that anyone heard anything over that. There was nothing you could do, Mee-Maw. None of this is your fault."

"It may seem that way, but I just can't shake the feeling that I should have known this was coming." She sat back in her chair and gazed up at the ceiling. "Never in a million years would I imagine that Victoria could do something like this."

"You think it was Victoria?" Ally's eyes widened. "You think she murdered him over Christmas decorations?"

"I don't know for sure, of course. But like you said, Martin's decorations were all knocked over and some were even broken. I hardly think that Martin would let that go. He probably went over there and confronted her. Maybe she got so angry that she came back with a weapon." She shuddered at the thought. "To think I could have been living so close to a murderer makes me feel just terrible."

"We don't know that for sure. It seems like a very weak motive for murder." Ally stood up and began to pace back and forth. She always liked to be on the move when she was trying to figure things out. "What about Trudy? You said she left him? Obviously, they had some kind of big fight. Maybe she tried to come home, and he wouldn't let her?"

"Trudy?" Charlotte scrunched up her nose. "She's so tiny. So thin, and so small, I just don't see how she could do that. She's always been so sweet."

"She might not have had a choice. Martin was so angry, maybe when she came home they fought, and in fear of her life she attacked. We don't know what might have really happened." Ally sat back down with a huff. "It's possible though, I think."

"You're right it is. I just find the whole scenario hard to believe. They seemed to love each other. I mean, I know that Martin had his moments, but he could be very sweet at other times. Even when he was angry he still seemed to be okay towards Trudy." She tapped her fingertips on the arm of her chair. "So as of now we have two possibilities. Victoria might have lost it, or Trudy might have killed him and taken off. Ally?" Her voice trailed off as she saw the look on her granddaughter's face. "Ally, what's wrong?"

"Mee-Maw, this happened practically right next door to you. I don't even want to think about something so horrible happening to you. What if it was random? What if someone just decided to kill Martin, and what if they're not done?" Ally asked, she tried to hide the worry in her voice. She knew she needed to be strong for her grandmother. "I'm staying here with you tonight. Or you can come to the cottage, whichever you prefer."

"No, I don't think I should leave here, it might send the wrong message. But you can stay if you want." She smiled some. "I would like that."

"Good, because you're not getting rid of me. I've already fed the pets." Ally frowned. "I just wish that Luke was here. At least he would keep us up to date on what's going on with the case. I doubt the chief is going to do that for us. He seems to have a problem with me."

"I noticed that, too. Maybe just because you're dating one of his detectives?" Charlotte raised an eyebrow.

"Maybe." Ally sighed and then turned towards

her grandmother. "I'm going to double-check the lock. You should get some rest."

"I'm not sure I can. But I'll try." Charlotte stood up from her chair and made her way into her room. As soon as she closed her eyes, she saw Martin, not as she'd found him, but as the angry man she'd seen earlier in the evening. Was it possible that he'd attacked his wife and she'd fought back? Before that encounter with him she never would have believed it. But as she fell asleep, she saw the anger in his eyes.

CHAPTER 5

When Charlotte opened her eyes the next morning, she had a few blissful seconds of ignorance. Then the memories of the night before crashed through her mind and ruffled every nerve in her body. Martin was dead, she was a suspect, and as far as she knew Trudy was missing. She heard the sound of the coffee pot brewing and knew that Ally was already up. Knowing her, she might not have slept at all. Charlotte wondered how she would handle the busy shop, and this on top of it. She hoped that the police might have solved the crime overnight. However, as she padded into the kitchen she could hear the morning news report. No leads, no explanations, suspect at large. She was sure that all of Freely Lakes would be in a tizzy about the possibility of an armed killer wandering the halls. If she was honest with herself, she felt a little scared. Not of the killer, but of what might happen if the police decided that she was the best suspect.

"Morning, Ally."

"Morning, Mee-Maw." She turned off the television and looked over at her grandmother. "Were you able to sleep?"

"Yes, I got some. What about you?" She met her eyes.

"A little, the couch is quite comfortable." Ally poured a cup of coffee for her, then set out the cream. "I got up a little while ago and started digging into what I could about Martin. However, there wasn't much to find. He's from Mainbry, but he lived in Freely for the past ten years, the last eight of those in Freely Lakes. He doesn't have much of an internet presence." Ally sat down beside Charlotte. "How are you feeling this morning? Maybe we should make an appointment with the doctor to have you checked out."

"Checked out for what?" She frowned. "It's not as if I was hurt."

"No, but you got a fright when you found Martin. It must have been stressful."

"I was just thinking the same thing about you

this morning. All of the stress of the holiday season, and now this on top of it." She gave Ally's hand a squeeze.

"Aw, Mee-Maw, you don't have to worry about that. I love working at the shop. And you and I both know we enjoy a mystery. I just wish it wasn't a murder mystery, and right around the holidays." She set a plate of toast in front of her grandmother. "Eat up."

"Thank you. You too."

"I'm joining you." She added toast to the table for herself.

"After breakfast, I know that you need to get to the shop, but I want to stop in and check on my friend Diana. She lives a few doors down from Martin and was friendly with Trudy. I'm worried that all of this will have her very shaken up." She frowned. "She's a bit nervous to begin with."

"Isn't she the one that bought the chocolates for her handmade giftboxes, yesterday?" Ally quirked an eyebrow.

"Yes, she is. She is so talented."

"I better go into the shop early. We have a ton of orders and deliveries to fill. Why don't you stay home today? I have Nina to help me out." She collected the plates and took them to the sink to wash them.

"And miss out on the gossip from Mrs. Cale, Mrs. Bing, and Mrs. White? Never!" She laughed a little. "Besides if I stay at Freely Lakes, I'm just going to go stir crazy. I'm sure everyone is going to stick close to home with everything that is happening." She stood up from the table and shooed Ally away from the sink. "You go on to the shop, I'll meet you there after I check on Diana. Then we can knock out some of the big orders that need to be done today. All right?" She eyed her for a moment. It was clear that it was not exactly a question.

"All right, that sounds good." She dried off her hands. "I need to stop at home first and feed Peaches and Arnold, then I'll head into the shop. But, Mee-Maw please, if anything strange happens, let me know right away. And be careful, okay?"

"I will be." She patted Ally's back. "You don't have to worry so much about me, remember?"

"I'll stop worrying about you, when you stop worrying about me." She kissed her grandmother's cheek.

On the way out the door Ally felt a sudden urge to stay. It seemed wrong not to keep an eye on her when there was a killer on the loose. But she also knew that her grandmother was never one to be scared off by anything. She wouldn't like Ally to follow her around like a babysitter. Ally wouldn't like anyone to do that to her, either. As she drove to the cottage, her thoughts churned with the possibilities of what might have happened to Martin. She'd heard many stories from her grandmother about the conflict between Martin and Victoria. It extended beyond just the holidays to other issues. But disputes between neighbors weren't that unusual, and didn't often lead to murder.

She parked in front of the cottage and unlocked the door to a cacophony of animal sounds.

"I know, I know, I've been gone too long." She sighed as she crouched down to greet the cat and the pig. They both picked a hand to lick and nuzzle. Ally couldn't help but laugh at the greeting. It did make her feel quite lucky to have them in her life. Once she fed them and made sure they had plenty of water for the day, she headed to her room to change. On the way back out she noticed that Arnold had dug his snout through her purse. He'd pushed a few letters and receipts out of it onto the floor.

"Arnold!" She frowned and gathered up the papers. "These are important." A few were invoices of orders from the shop, while another was a list of people she planned to send a card. As she looked at the list she was reminded of how late she was sending them. She shivered a little as she realized that both Victoria and Martin were on that list. Would she be sending a card to Trudy? Or Victoria? She doubted it now. Once she had all of the papers back in her purse she headed out the door again. It was too cold to bring Peaches and Arnold to the pen out back. She would have to make it up to them by bringing home some special treats, as she knew they were missing their outings and interaction with the people of Blue River.

~

*C*harlotte placed her hand on the doorknob and wondered if she should really turn it. Once she stepped outside there was no turning back, she knew that. She'd be stared at by her neighbors, and Diana might not even open her door for her. But she still felt an obligation to check on her friend. As far as she knew Diana had no one else to turn to, and she was quite worried about her. She and Trudy were quite friendly and she only lived a few doors down from Martin and Trudy. She turned the knob, and stepped out into the hall. Luckily, there was no one else around.

The police tape still surrounded Martin's apartment. It felt strange not to hear any Christmas music. All of the decorations were gone. She wasn't sure if the police had taken them for evidence, or just out of courtesy, but either way she was relieved not to see them. When she reached Diana's door, she hesitated. Would she even want to see her? Would it frighten her that someone was knocking? After a deep breath, she knocked. A few seconds later the door swung open and Diana stood before her. Or at least she attempted to stand. She swayed, and seemed to be on the verge of tears.

"Diana? Are you okay?"

"Yes, I'm sorry." She cleared her throat. "I don't know who I was expecting, but it wasn't you."

"I just wanted to check on you. I know that with everything that happened you have to be shaken. I am." She met her eyes. "Can I come in?"

"Oh no, not now." She sighed and leaned against the door frame. "Everything is a mess. I'm just not fit to entertain. I appreciate you checking on me, though. It means a lot to me."

"Of course. If you feel like you want some company, I don't care what your apartment looks like, and you can always come over to mine." Char-lotte bit into her bottom lip for a moment as she considered whether she should say more. Her curiosity prevented her from being silent. "Did you hear anything last night? See anything strange?"

"Goodness no. The police asked me that, too. I just delivered the gifts, came back here, you came and dropped off the chocolates and I went to bed. It wasn't until I heard you screaming that I knew something was wrong. That's why I called the police." She clutched at her neck. "Oh, Charlotte I was so scared, I thought something had happened to you."

"I'm so glad you had the presence of mind to call. I couldn't even think straight to get to my phone. Thank you for that, Diana." She held out her hand to her. Diana took it, though hers trembled. "You're a good friend."

"So are you, that's why I was so worried about you." She squeezed her hand in return. "I thought something terrible had happened, and it had, but I'm ashamed to say I was a little relieved when I found out it was Martin and not you."

"Don't be ashamed. I understand." Charlotte swallowed hard. "I'm really worried about Trudy. I thought maybe she had been hurt, too, but there's no sign of her. You haven't heard from her or seen her, have you?"

"Not since yesterday, no. I saw her in the morning, but not after that. I just can't believe this happened. Poor Trudy. When she finds out, she's going to be so upset." She pressed her hand to her cheek and shuddered. "The shock of it might just put her in the hospital."

"Yes, it might." Charlotte studied her for a moment, then brought a smile to her lips. "My offer stands. If you need anything at all, just let me know. Okay?"

"I'm the one that should be offering you things. After all, you had to endure the shock of finding him. I'm so sorry about that, Charlotte. I'm sure it can't be easy to live with that." She shook her head slowly back and forth as if she was in her own state of shock. "I hate to even think of it."

"It was quite a shock, but I'm okay now. I'm more interested in finding out what happened to him. Someone had to have seen or heard something. I know the police are looking into Victoria." She pursed her lips.

"Oh, you know that, do you?" The voice that came from behind Charlotte made her blood run cold. She reluctantly turned to face Victoria. There was no way to pretend she hadn't said what she said.

Victoria's cheeks were bright red, a stark contrast to the white hair piled up on the top of her head in a messy bun. Though Victoria was about the same age as Charlotte, she always struck her as much younger. A permanent cheerleader who hadn't aged much past thirty.

"Victoria, I just meant that they were interested in speaking with you." Charlotte willed her heart to slow down.

"I'm sure that's what you meant. You can tell all of the busybodies out there that I had nothing to do with this, Charlotte. Just because I didn't like the man's taste in decorations doesn't mean that I would kill him. The one they should be looking into is his wife. She's the one with a good reason to kill him." She rolled her eyes and stormed off back to her apartment. Charlotte turned back to Diana, but she had already scurried back into her apartment. Still stunned by Victoria's presence, Charlotte tried to piece her thoughts together. Did Victoria know something more about Trudy than she was letting on? She summoned determination and walked up to Victoria's door. When she knocked, she was certain that Victoria wouldn't answer. But a second later, she did.

"What do you want?" She glared at Charlotte. "I'm sure you're the one that told the cops all about me having a problem with Martin."

"No, I didn't." She took a deep breath. "I want to apologize. I shouldn't have been gossiping like that. I don't normally, and I'm sorry that I was. It's just I'm the one who found Martin, and I've been upset ever since."

"I'm sure you are. From what I hear, you're just as much a suspect as I am. Don't think that sweet and innocent act is going to help you get away with anything." She eyed Charlotte with disgust. "I always knew you were two-faced."

"I'm not that at all, Victoria. I'm just trying to understand what happened here. Do you know of anyone who might have had a problem with Martin?" She hoped steering the conversation away from herself would calm them both down.

"Like I said, you're better off talking to Trudy. She wasn't as innocent as you think, you know? When you live across from someone you get to know things. Like who goes to play golf every Saturday, and who shows up after he leaves." She wiggled her eyebrows. "Trudy wasn't letting anything slow her down."

"Are you serious? She was having an affair?" Charlotte's eyes widened. "With whom?"

"This would be the time when you should ask yourself, Charlotte, do you really want to know?" She leaned closer. "Because some things are better left a mystery."

"What are you talking about, Victoria?" Charlotte narrowed her eyes. "You're just making all of this up, aren't you?"

"Believe what you want. It makes no difference to me." She pushed the door shut. Charlotte heard the lock slide closed. Her nerves were on edge, but she knew she wouldn't get another word out of her.

CHAPTER 6

*A*lly unlocked the door to the shop and stepped inside. A wave of exhaustion carried over her, but as it faded she tried to focus on the orders that needed to be filled. She was engrossed in creating a batch of chocolates when she heard a knock on the front door. It startled her as she'd slipped into the quiet space in her mind that she sometimes retreated to while working. Once she realized where she was, she thought perhaps a customer wanted an early treat. She headed to the front door with a glance at the clock along the way. It was still an hour before opening. Through the door she saw a familiar face, but it only caused her more apprehension. It was the chief. She was tempted not to unlock the door. Instead, she opened it and greeted him with a smile.

"Good morning, would you like some coffee?"

"No thank you." He stepped in through the door without being invited. "I'd like to speak to Charlotte."

"She's not here yet. I'm sure she'll be here soon." Ally's heartbeat quickened. Was he there to arrest her? "You know she had nothing to do with this."

"I don't know that, actually. I'd like to know that, as that would wipe a suspect off my list, but I can't know that because she's not here to speak to, is she?" He crossed his arms. "I'm sure you won't mind if I wait?"

"You're welcome to stay as long as you need. I do have some chocolates I'm working on in the back. Would you like to join me?" She gestured towards the door that led to the kitchen.

"No thanks. I'm allergic to chocolate."

"What?" She nearly choked on her words.

"It's a joke." He arched an eyebrow, though his expression did not change in the least. "Listen, I'm not here to give your grandmother a hard time. But I have to do my job, or actually, the job of my employees who aren't here right now to do it. I'd be more than happy to stop bothering her if she can prove to me that she was nowhere near Martin when he was killed. So, was she with you around eight o'clock?"

"No." Ally frowned. "Is that when he was killed?"

"Yes. Approximately between seven-thirty and eight-thirty. I have witnesses who saw your grandmother arguing with Martin a little after seven." He held her gaze. "Do you suggest I just ignore that?"

"No, sir. I wouldn't suggest that. But I do think you're wasting your time looking into my grandmother. What about Victoria? She was known to have a problem with Martin. She had a fight with him about his decorations and music almost every single day. Are you investigating her?" She tried to fight the fear that his words stirred within her.

"We're looking into everyone who might have had a problem with Martin. But so far, at the moment, your grandmother was the last person to see him alive, and that means a lot. You just let me do my job, and I will get to the bottom of this, I can assure you of that." He glanced at his watch. "How long do you think she will be?"

Ally looked up at the clock. She knew that her grandmother would arrive any second, but she didn't want to tell him that. Maybe if he thought she would be a long time he wouldn't stick around to bother her. Before she could decide how to answer, her grandmother pushed open the door to the shop.

"Sorry I took so long, Ally, I was checking on Diana, and then you wouldn't believe it, I ran into Victoria!"

"Oh?" The chief spun on his heel to face her. "What did she have to say?"

"I'm sorry, I didn't realize…" Charlotte's face flushed as she looked at him. "She just said that she had nothing to do with Martin's death."

"Hmm, same thing she told me." He pushed his hat up about an inch on his head. "Same story you told me, too. I guess no one killed him. There's no crime here after all. We can all go home." He clapped his hands.

Ally and Charlotte stared at him, horrified.

"This is nothing to joke about." Charlotte put her hands on her hips. "Martin was my friend. Whoever did this to him deserves to pay."

"He was your friend? Or is Trudy more your friend? Maybe you got tired of seeing him push her around? Was that it? You decided to take matters into your own hands?" He moved closer to her, placing himself directly between the two women.

"No, of course not. I've never seen Martin hurt Trudy. If I had, I would have turned him in myself."

She narrowed her eyes. "I did not kill anyone, Chief, no matter how you want to spin it. You can suspect me all you want, but at some point you're going to realize that I am an asset. I am going to be working just as hard as you to figure out what happened here. Anything you have to say, I'll listen, any questions you want to ask, I'll answer. But keep in mind, at the end of all of this, we're still going to have to live in the same town, and see each other on a regular basis. So please be careful with accusations that you can't take back."

"I should be careful." He eyed her for a long moment. The pulsation of the vein in his forehead eased some. "Because I'm not one to have the wool pulled over my eyes. I know that you and Jeff are close. Maybe, he didn't like you talking to Martin so much? Maybe, he had a reason to be jealous?" He tapped his fingertip to the side of his head. "I'm always looking for the motive, Charlotte, and when I find it, I'll make sure it's correct. Until then, you should be just as careful as me, because yes, when this is all over, you're going to have to deal with me, one way or the other." As he turned and left the shop, Charlotte felt her hope of this case getting solved smoothly go right out the door with him. It didn't matter to him that she'd lived in the town for decades, or that she'd never had a smudge on her record. All that mattered to him was finding the killer, and if she fit that bill, she guessed that he wouldn't hesitate to put her in handcuffs.

"Mee-Maw? Are you okay?" Ally asked.

"Yes." She shuddered then took a deep breath. "I'm just glad he's gone."

"Ugh, he's just awful isn't he?" Ally glared at the door. "I wish I would have said what was on my mind."

"Ally, if you did that, we'd both be in his sights. I think we just need to keep a low profile. As long as he is determined to find something to pin on me, he'll be sniffing around me. Let him, I have nothing to hide."

"But you also have no alibi." Ally frowned. "He told me the time of death is between seven-thirty and eight-thirty. You were home alone during that time. There's no way to prove otherwise. There are no cameras in the hallways."

"Maybe not, but I don't need to prove it. All I need to do is find the real killer. That will clear up any suspicion of me."

Ally nodded, but she was still concerned.

A few minutes later there was another knock on the door. It was about ten minutes before opening time. Ally stepped out of the kitchen to see who it was, while Charlotte continued to fill molds. When she saw Nina through the door she felt a sense of relief. For a second there, she thought the chief had returned. When she unlocked the door, Nina greeted her with a small smile.

"Morning, Ally."

"Good morning." Ally left the door unlocked since it was just about time to open. "Mee-Maw's in the back working on some chocolates. We got a late start today."

"She's here?" Nina hesitated near the door.

"Yes." Ally glanced over her shoulder at her. "Is everything okay?"

"Oh sure, I guess I just thought she might want the day off, with everything that happened." She shrugged as she walked towards the broom in the corner behind the register.

"So, you've heard?" Ally worked on opening up the register.

"It was all over the news, but it's all around town that Charlotte was the one who found him." She cleared her throat. "How terrible."

"Yes, well, Mee-Maw is never one to take a day off. It was hard for her, but she's doing better today." She popped open the drawer to count the money.

"That's good." Nina busied herself with sweeping the floor.

"Oh, do you have that paperwork?" Ally looked up from the register.

"Darn, I forgot it. I'm sorry. I can go back home and get it if you want."

"No, it's okay. Just bring it with you tomorrow, it'll be fine." Ally brushed her hair back into a pony-tail and began to wipe down the counters.

CHAPTER 7

*A*lly had just gotten all of the sample trays filled when the door swung open, and in walked Mrs. Bing, Mrs. Cale, and Mrs. White.

"Good morning, ladies." Ally spared them a half-smile. None of them returned the smile, or the greeting, but Mrs. Bing did snatch up a piece of chocolate from the sample tray.

"I'd say it's a terrible morning." Mrs. White clutched her purse. Her cheeks looked flushed, but only because of the makeup she wore. Where there was little makeup her skin appeared pale. Ally wondered if she wasn't feeling well.

"Yes, I guess it isn't a good one." Ally stepped out from behind the register and regarded the three women with interest. If anyone would have some gossip to share about the murder, it would be them. "I guess you've heard?"

"Who hasn't?" Mrs. Cale fluffed the loose curls at the end of her hair. "Between the news and breakfast club this morning, I don't think anyone could have missed it."

"It's a terrible, terrible thing." Ally shook her head. She noticed that Nina lingered nearby.

"What I don't understand is why it took her so long." Mrs. White waved her hand dismissively.

"Took who so long?" Ally narrowed her eyes.

"Trudy, of course. She's still missing, isn't she?" Mrs. White looked at the other two women, then back at Ally. "That's clearly a sign of guilt, isn't it?"

"I'm not sure if she's missing, or she just doesn't know what happened, yet." Ally rested her hands on the counter and studied Mrs. White. "But as far as I know the police aren't close to making an arrest."

"Oh, she knows." Mrs. Bing tucked another piece of chocolate in her mouth, then talked around it. "Who can blame her? Whatever he said, went, and she never got a say in any of it. She didn't want to move, that was for sure, but he didn't care one bit about what she wanted."

"Who could blame her for murdering her

husband?" Mrs. Cale gasped. "What a horrible thing to say. There's no excuse for murder."

"No, there's not." Mrs. Bing nodded as her voice shifted into a calmer tone. "However, sometimes a person just snaps. Trudy has been putting up with Martin for years, and I imagine that she just had enough."

"Wait a minute, they were planning to move?" Ally shook her head. "I didn't know anything about that."

"Sure, the apartment was listed. Martin wanted to spend a couple of years on cruise ships and then maybe buy a place in the mountains. Trudy hated boats. Can you believe that he wanted to force her to spend years on something she hated?" Mrs. Bing scrunched up her nose. "Just another form of torment I suppose."

"Trudy tried to talk him out of selling, but he wouldn't listen. Everything's in his name. She had no way to stop it. Maybe she just panicked." Mrs. White sighed and her eyes gained a faraway look. "I know it's not right, and there's no excuse, but a part of me understands why she might have done it. You'll probably never experience this, Ally, but women of our generation, we spent most of our lives dependent on the men in our lives. It was just the way things were done. Then you get to our age, and if you're not a widow, those men still have full control over your life."

"That's true." Mrs. Cale nodded. "Before my Henry passed away, every single Sunday we had to eat at the buffet. I hated eating at the buffet, but he drove, and he paid the bill, so we ate at the buffet."

"That's not exactly what I meant." Mrs. White smiled.

"But it's the same thing. Your freedom of choice doesn't exist when someone else has control. Not me, never me." Mrs. Bing plucked another chocolate.

"So, Trudy and Martin weren't happy? I really had the wrong impression." Ally frowned as she realized how much she missed about their relationship. Maybe her instincts weren't as trustworthy as she thought.

"I wouldn't say they weren't happy." Mrs. Bing shrugged. "Every couple has their problems. In general, they seemed to get along well. But when all this started about selling the apartment, that's when everything seemed to change."

"Seemed to change is the key there." Mrs. White narrowed her eyes. "She's always been intimidated by him, I wouldn't be surprised if something else was going on behind the scenes."

"Rumors." Mrs. Cale wagged her finger. "Nothing but rumors. A person's personal life, is their personal life. Until it's splashed across the news of course." She sighed.

"I'm sure as soon as Trudy reappears all of this will be resolved." Ally added some more chocolates to the sample tray. "She's probably just gone somewhere to cool off, and maybe she'll have more information for the police when she gets back."

"I hope you're right, Ally," Mrs. White said. "Even if it's not Trudy, it's usually someone close to home."

"I agree." Nina walked over and looked at Mrs. White. "The investigators should look close to home. The murderer is often the obvious suspect."

Just then the door to the shop swung open. Charlotte stepped out from the kitchen in the same moment. She smiled at the three women huddled around the sample tray, then waved to the woman that stepped through the door.

"Beth, it's good to see you."

"You too, Charlotte." Beth walked towards her with a strained expression. "I was going to call when

I heard, but I thought stopping in might be better. I wasn't sure if you would be here, though."

"Yes, this is my home away from home." Charlotte smiled a bit. "Thanks for checking on me."

"I'm just glad that you're okay." She lowered her voice. "Did you hear Mary's apartment was broken into early this morning?"

"Mary's?" Charlotte's eyes widened. Mary was a quiet woman who sat a few tables away from her at the gift making class. "How terrible and unusual. I can't remember the last time I heard about a break-in at Freely Lakes."

"I know, it has everyone on edge. People are worried that it might have been Martin's killer." She shivered. "The very thought makes me so nervous."

"Mary's okay, though?" Charlotte met her eyes.

"Shaken up, but okay. We all need to be more careful." Her worried eyes passed over the three women near the counter as well.

"Yes, we do." Mrs. White nodded. "Lock your doors, always." She eyed Mrs. Bing for a moment. "That means you, too."

"Okay, I know, sometimes I forget!" Mrs. Bing blushed. "I'll be more careful."

"Here, let me get you some of the chocolates I made with those molds that you gave me." Charlotte stepped behind the counter and began packing up a box. When she returned with it, Beth smiled with gratitude.

"Thank you, Charlotte. This will certainly brighten my day." She frowned. "I'm trying to decide whether to cancel class tonight."

"I don't think you should. We all need something to distract ourselves from all of this. If you have it, I can assure you that I will be there." She met her eyes. "Martin would have wanted us to continue on with our holiday activities. It was his favorite time of year."

"Yes, I guess you're right about that." She nodded to the others, then left the shop.

"The nerve she has." Mrs. White announced as soon as the door closed. She gave a sharp shake of her head.

"What do you mean?" Ally walked around the counter towards her.

"Oh, trust me, there was no love lost between her and Martin. I'm surprised the two of them were able to operate within any distance of each other. It didn't used to be that way." She raised an eyebrow as she looked at Mrs. Bing. "Remember?"

"Oh, I do." Mrs. Bing nodded. "They started that business together. The travel agency in Mainbry, where they are from. It was supposed to be very successful. But according to what I've been told, Beth took off with his investment. The business collapsed, and Martin nearly lost everything."

"Oh no, no. That's not how I heard it." Mrs. Cale popped a chocolate in her mouth, sucked on it, and waited for everyone to turn their attention on her. "I heard that Martin was the one who bailed on the business, when he wanted her to invest more money to expand and she refused. Beth lost everything she had, was almost homeless. But that was all so many years ago. Really, things do have to be forgiven eventually. Don't you think?"

"Maybe so." Mrs. White pursed her lips. "I'd never heard that version of the story, now I'm not sure what to believe."

"Isn't that how most rumors go?" Ally frowned. "I suppose we should be careful what news we're sharing."

"Yes." Mrs. Bing picked up a few more chocolates. "Thank you for the treats, Ally."

"You're welcome." Ally smiled at her.

As the three left the shop, Ally looked over at her grandmother.

"Do you know anything about the issue between Beth and Martin?"

"No, nothing." Charlotte's eyes widened. "It's amazing to me that I never knew about it. I remember that they were going into business together, but that was around the time your mother became ill, and I lost track of so many things during that time." Her cheeks flushed. "I suppose that since it was so long ago it likely didn't have anything to do with Martin's death."

"Maybe, but maybe not. If Martin was planning on selling his apartment, and Beth really did lose money in the business, maybe she hoped to recover some of that money from him after the sale." Ally lifted an eyebrow. "I think it's a possibility."

"But then why would she kill him?" Charlotte asked.

"True, that doesn't make sense." Ally nodded. "Maybe she inherited something."

"Maybe."

"Ally, aren't there several orders to fill?" Nina started towards the kitchen. "Would you like me to start working on them?" She barely looked in Ally's direction.

"Not just yet, Nina, there are too many cooling that need to be packed. If you'd like you can replenish the sample trays." She studied her for a moment. Something felt different about Nina, though she couldn't quite place what it was.

"Sure." She stepped into the back to retrieve more chocolates. As Ally turned back towards her grandmother, the door of the shop swung open again.

"Charlotte!" Jeff rushed through the door. "Why didn't you call me?" He walked straight over to her.

"Oh well, I didn't want to bother you." She smiled as he looked into her eyes. "I meant to call you this morning, but things have been a bit busy."

"Why don't you take a break, Mee-Maw?" Ally tilted her head towards Jeff. "It seems like he'd really like to talk with you."

"I guess you're right. Thanks." Charlotte nodded and gave Ally a brief smile before turning back to Jeff. "Why don't we go get some lunch?"

"That's a great idea." He nodded and guided her through the door.

Once Ally and Nina were alone in the shop, Ally noticed the quiet. Nina had barely spoken to her all day. Normally Nina was a chatterbox.

"Is everything okay, Nina?" Ally walked over to her. "If this is too much, we can cut back the hours a bit."

"It's not the hours." She crossed her arms as she studied Ally. "I'm just surprised that you're so comfortable with having Charlotte here."

"I'm sorry? Why wouldn't I be? She's my grandmother. She owns this place." Ally gazed at her, confused.

"I just think having a murder suspect here is probably bad for business." Nina shrugged.

"First of all, Mee-Maw is not a murder suspect, because she's innocent. Secondly, I would never show anything but support for her. I'm really surprised by this, Nina. If you feel uncomfortable working around her maybe you should leave." A quick anger built up inside of Ally. She'd never imagined she'd have to defend her grandmother to her friend.

"Ally, calm down. I wasn't accusing her of anything. I just thought it was bad for business. I mean it's not as if she couldn't stay home for a few days. It just seemed like a poor decision on your part to encourage her to be here." She licked her lips. "If you want me to go, I'll go. But I'd rather stay."

"Maybe you should go for today. Let's just pick things up again tomorrow. I know my nerves are on edge." She turned away from Nina. Maybe she was being overly sensitive, maybe she'd misinterpreted what the woman said to her.

"Okay, I'll go. I'm sorry, Ally, I didn't mean to upset you." Nina gathered her things, then left the shop.

Alone in the shop, Ally felt anxious. Something about the exchange with Nina made her wonder if she knew the woman at all. When her cell phone rang in the quiet store it made her jump. She answered it as soon as she saw who it was.

"Oh, Luke, it's so good to hear from you." She frowned as she saw a group of people heading towards the shop. "I'm sorry, I don't think I'm going to be able to talk right now."

"Just listen for a moment. I heard about what happened, and that Charlotte is a suspect. You need to be careful, Ally. Someone is giving the chief anonymous information about Charlotte, false information, that he could use to build a case against her. Watch your step. Understand?"

"Yes, but who?" Her heart raced as the door swung open.

"I don't know who. I'm trying to get back, but it's impossible with the weather approaching. Just stay on your toes, and I will do whatever I can from here. Tell Charlotte to be careful who she trusts."

"I will. Thank you, Luke. Love you."

"Love you, too."

As she hung up the phone, her stomach twisted. Who could be telling lies about her grandmother? Was the real killer trying to frame her? What lies were they? She didn't have time to think about it, as the group entered the shop and she shifted her attention to them. As much as she wanted to know more about what Luke had to say, she still had to run the shop. However, it was impossible for her to concentrate. After she burned the chocolate she melted, and mixed up an order she'd spent almost an hour putting together, she felt tears threaten. If the chief had it in for her grandmother, how would she ever be able to protect her?

CHAPTER 8

*O*nce Charlotte and Jeff were settled at the diner, Charlotte was eager to look at the menu.

"Honestly, I know I shouldn't be able to eat, but I'm starving." She looked up from the menu.

"I bet you haven't eaten in quite some time if you really think about it."

"I didn't finish my toast this morning." She rubbed a hand across her forehead. "I just wish all of this was already over. Poor Martin." She sighed.

"Get some food in your belly, it'll help you feel better." He gestured for the waitress to come over. As they placed their orders, Charlotte recalled what Victoria said to her that morning. What had she meant by it?

"I know you must have so much on your mind,

Charlotte." Jeff looked into her eyes. "I'm here if you want to talk. About anything."

"Mostly, I want to talk about Victoria. I just can't shake the memory of the way she looked at Martin when they argued. I really think she wanted to tear into him." She frowned. "I know that doesn't make her a killer, but I can't help but wonder if maybe she snapped. I mean, who else would destroy his Christmas decorations? I saw them torn apart, apparently just about an hour before he may have been killed, or even less. I can't help but think he went to confront her, and maybe she came to his apartment and decided to end things once and for all."

"I had a terrible neighbor once. He kept stealing things off my porch. At first it was no big deal to me. He'd take my newspaper, or a flower pot. But then he started taking my tools, even one of my chairs, and I just couldn't keep letting it slide. Every time I confronted him, he insisted it wasn't him, and that I was nuts. So, I put a camera up. I didn't tell him about it. The next day, another of my chairs went missing. I checked the camera, and clear as day, this man took the chair right off my porch. I went to him with the recording, and threatened to call the police. But instead of doing that I made him promise to stay off my property. From that day on he never set foot on my property."

"You never called the police?" Charlotte studied him curiously.

"No. I didn't want to put him in jail, I just wanted him to stop stealing from me. Some people have mental problems, you know. I'm certainly no one to judge anyone else. I have my own issues. The point is, a camera took care of the problem." He shrugged. "Maybe Martin should have tried it."

"Maybe he did." Charlotte snapped her fingers. "I wonder if he might have hidden a camera. It's a long shot, but possible, right?"

"I would think the police would have found it, but it's possible." He shifted some in his seat. "I wonder if he would have told Trudy."

"We'll never know if she doesn't show up." She sighed.

"She'll be back." He sat back as their food was delivered.

"How can you be so certain?" She met his eyes as the waitress set her soup down in front of her.

"She's not one to run and hide." He smiled at the waitress and thanked her.

"I didn't realize you knew her well." Charlotte

had seen them exchange greetings, but it never went further than that.

"Yes, we're friends." He glanced up at her. "I can tell you, she's no murderer."

"Not even if Martin was pushing her around?" She noticed a flicker of shame cross his features.

"They had their differences, but Martin and her got along well. I don't think he ever got violent with her." He picked up his fork, but didn't touch his food. "At least she never told me he did."

"But you're not convinced?" Her heart skipped a beat as she realized that Jeff knew her neighbors better than she did. But how?

"Martin had some harsh qualities about him. His tone, his mannerisms, they all indicate that he might have been violent, but lots of people are brusque and loud. It's hard to make that judgment. He was always caring towards Trudy from what I could tell." He swept his fork through his chicken and took a bite.

"How do you know Trudy so well?" She watched as he took another bite of his chicken.

"Oh, we had a shared interest." He picked up his glass and took a long swallow of his water.

"What shared interest?" Charlotte's head began to swirl. How could there be so much she didn't know about Jeff? She thought she'd gotten to know him very well.

"I'd rather not say." His cheeks flushed. "The point is, she didn't do this. I know she didn't."

"Well, someone did." She could hear the tension in her voice. "And the chief seems to think it was me."

"That's ridiculous." He tossed down his fork. "Where did he get his badge? Out of a cereal box?"

"Perhaps." She smiled slightly as she eyed her food.

"Aren't you going to eat?" He looked across the table at her with concern.

"I'm not so hungry anymore." She pushed the plate away.

"Charlotte? What's wrong?" He took her hand in his. She gazed into his eyes and hoped that the suspicion that stirred within her wasn't warranted.

"I think it's all just setting in. Will you excuse me? I need to use the restroom." She stood up from the table.

"Sure, of course." He watched her as she headed for the back hallway.

As Charlotte passed the table closest to the restrooms, she overheard an interesting comment.

"Yes, Benjamin's apartment was broken into

early this morning. Apparently, nothing of value was taken, and he slept through the whole thing."

"Then how did he know there was a break-in?" The woman on the other side of the table leaned closer to the first woman.

"Because his kitchen had been rummaged through, and a few kitchen items were taken, they were worthless, though. Can you imagine? Someone breaks in just to go through your kitchen and steal a few worthless things? Why would anyone do that?"

"I don't know, but apparently the same thing happened to Mary. You know what good security they have at Freely Lakes. I've heard some rumors saying that it must have been an inside job. Someone who lived there. Same with Martin's death." She clucked her tongue. "What is this town coming to?"

"Now, now. We still have much less crime than other places."

Charlotte continued on before she could get pulled into the conversation. Two break-ins? That was unheard of in Blue River. She couldn't help but wonder if they were somehow connected to Martin's murder. Mary and Benjamin hadn't been harmed, but maybe Martin had fought back? When she returned to the table, she was still lost in thought.

"I bet this will cheer you up." Jeff smiled as she sat back down. "I got a special delivery yesterday."

"You did?" She focused in on him. She hadn't forgotten that he was acting strangely.

"Your friend Diana dropped off a box of candies from Charlotte's Chocolate Heaven." He smacked his lips. "I didn't have the heart to tell her that I get as many treats as I want for free." He winked.

"What, you haven't been paying?" She grinned. "Did you see how lovely her painted boxes are?"

"Yes, I did. I thought about keeping it, but I owed a birthday gift to a friend, Michael, so I passed it along." He shrugged.

"You re-gifted?" Charlotte gasped along with a laugh. "How could you?"

"Look, it's not something I do all of the time, but I forgot about it and it did save me from having to do a last-minute shop. Your candies are better than anything I could have picked up at the store. Hopefully she won't find out." He grimaced.

"Oh, she probably won't. She had quite a long list of people she was handing out the gifts to. I'm sure that she won't realize you gave Michael the gift." She frowned. "I just realized something."

"What's that?" He held her gaze.

"There have been two break-ins, one at Mary's,

and one at Benjamin's. They're both in the gift making class with me at Freely Lakes. It's open to all residents. Do you think that could be coincidence?" She considered it for a moment.

"Is it a full class?" He finished the last bite of his food.

"Yes, it is."

"Then it could be a coincidence." He set his fork down. "Are you sure you're not going to eat?"

"Maybe I will." Charlotte picked up her spoon and sunk it into her soup.

～

*B*y the time her grandmother returned from lunch, Ally was desperate for her help. She was buried in orders, and had to set up appointments for a few customers to pick up their chocolates later as she ran out of their favorite kind. She'd never felt so overwhelmed at the shop before. She realized that she shouldn't have asked Nina to leave.

"Ally? What's happened here?" Charlotte picked up some napkins that were scattered across the floor, then gazed at the empty display shelves.

"There was quite a crowd." Ally brushed her

hair back from her eyes. It had come free from her ponytail at some point and she hadn't had time to fix it. "It was crazy."

"Where's Nina?" Charlotte glanced around the shop.

"I sent her home." Ally's jaw rippled as she tried not to think about the conversation they'd had.

"What? Why?" Charlotte cleaned up some more napkins, then started towards the kitchen. "Do you have any batches going?"

"Two, I just got behind is all, Mee-Maw, it happens." She didn't realize how sharp she was being until her grandmother walked over to her with a stern look.

"Ally, tell me what is really going on. Why did you send Nina home?"

"Mee-Maw, I'd rather not say." She frowned.

Charlotte recalled Jeff saying the exact same thing not long before. Why was everyone keeping secrets from her?

"Ally, tell me!"

"We need to talk, Mee-Maw, Luke called and…"

"One thing at a time." Charlotte walked over to the door of the shop and turned the lock, then she flipped the sign to closed. Ally knew she was determined as she never closed the shop during regular hours unless it was serious. "I can live with the stares, and the comments, from other people. But I will not tolerate you hiding things from me, Ally. We're in this together, remember?"

"Yes, I remember." Ally sighed. "I sent her home because she thought it was wrong for you to be here. That it was bad for business."

"Well, she was right about that. If people suspect I was involved in Martin's death then they might not come in." Charlotte touched her granddaughter's cheek. "But I can see that it upset you."

"I thought she was my friend, Mee-Maw. I thought we had a connection." She shook her head. "I guess I was wrong. But that's not important now. Luke told me that someone is giving the police false information about you that is making you their main suspect. I'm so worried that they're going to think they have enough to make an arrest."

"Okay, okay, deep breaths." Charlotte wasn't sure if she was instructing Ally or herself to calm down. "The chief may be a tough cookie, but he's not stupid. I'm sure he'll see through any lies that are being spread about me."

"But who would spread them? Whoever it is must be the killer. I think you're being framed." Ally took her grandmother's hands and looked into her eyes. "Luke said he's trying to get back here, but that we need to watch our step until then. He's stuck, because there's a snow storm coming in, and no flights out."

"We'll be careful, we're always careful. It doesn't matter what lies are told, if we find out the truth. I think I may have something to go on."

"You do?"

"Both Mary and Benjamin's apartments were broken into."

"Really!" Ally's eyes widened. "That can't be a coincidence."

"No, I don't think so either, but I think that's where we need to start, with the break-ins. I think maybe whoever is doing the break-ins started with Martin, and for some reason they killed him. If we can figure out who is behind them then I'm betting we'll have our killer."

"How are we going to do that?" Ally leaned back against the counter. "If Luke was here maybe we could get some inside information."

"I say we go speak to Mary and to Benjamin. That's a start." She walked back towards the door to unlock it. "But first, you need to call Nina and get her back in here. She's entitled to her opinion. It does bother me a bit, but we need her help." She looked back at Ally. "Sometimes you have to set aside your personal feelings and do what's best for the shop."

Ally nodded, though she didn't entirely agree. She knew her grandmother was trying to impart some great wisdom upon her, but at the same time she no longer trusted Nina. Still, she dialed her number and when she picked up, she asked her to come back to the shop. She even apologized for asking her to leave. She knew it would be tense between them, but Charlotte was right, without the extra help the business might suffer, and they would have no free time to investigate Martin's murder. With Charlotte's freedom on the line, she wasn't willing to take any chances. It made her nervous to think that Nina would be back in the shop with them, as she wasn't sure that she could be trusted. But customers flooded the shop within minutes, and as she and Charlotte tried to keep up, she was glad that Nina was on her way in.

During a quiet moment, Charlotte met her eyes.

"When Nina gets here, I'm going to run out and see if I can catch Benjamin at his house. Is that okay?"

"Of course it is, Mee-Maw. Thank you so much for all of your help. I think it's pretty clear that I couldn't run this place without you." She frowned as she realized what a disaster she'd created by sending Nina home.

"Ally. Sweetheart." She cupped her cheek and met her eyes. "The only thing you're doing wrong is being so very hard on yourself. The shop has a life of its own, it will change its mood at a moment's notice. It's not your role to try to control it, but flow with it. You're doing an excellent job, and I couldn't be prouder, or happier that I had you to turn over the reins to. No one else could ever fill that role."

"Thanks, Mee-Maw." Ally breathed a sigh of relief, then shifted her attention to the next customer that walked through the door. Only it wasn't a customer, it was Nina.

"Hi Nina, bye Nina." Charlotte waved to her as she hurried past in the process of tossing her purse over her shoulder.

"Bye Charlotte." Nina watched her go, then turned to face Ally. "I know this is going to be awkward."

"It doesn't have to be." Ally used the most professional tone she could muster. "I hired you because I believed you would do a good job, and I still believe that. Trust me, there isn't going to be time for things to be awkward." She pointed to a large group of people who were just about to walk into the shop. "Let's get to our battle stations!"

Nina nodded, and stepped behind the counter. It was still a little awkward, but Ally had to admit that she was grateful to have Nina there.

CHAPTER 9

Charlotte decided not to call Benjamin before visiting him. She knew she could easily get his number from Beth, since she had the entire class roster. However, she thought it might be better not to let him know she was coming. As it was, she knew that rumors about her involvement in the murder were spreading through town, and though she wasn't sure if they had reached him yet, she didn't want to take any chances. Instead, she decided to pop up at his door. When she parked in front of his house, a flutter of uncertainty carried through her. Would he even open the door for her? His car was in the driveway, which indicated that he was home. As she approached the door, she tried to feel confident. It was hard to with suspicion hanging over her head. When she knocked on the door, she braced herself for his reaction.

"Hello?" He peered out through the screen door. "Charlotte? Right?"

"Right." She was relieved that he at least remembered her. "Sorry to bother you. I just wanted to check and see if you were all right."

"Isn't there a class tonight?" He studied her for a moment then invited her inside.

"Oh, I'm on my way. I just thought I'd stop by and see how you're doing. I heard your house was broken into this morning. Is that true?" She held his gaze.

"Yes, it was. It's the strangest thing. I almost felt silly about reporting it to the police since nothing valuable was taken. But someone did break in." He pointed to the damage on the door frame. "Forced their way in, whoever it was."

"Wow, that must have been so frightening." Charlotte wrung her hands. "I'm so sorry you experienced that."

"Not as frightening as what happened to you." He looked back at her. "You did find Martin, didn't you?" His tone changed as he brought up the topic. She guessed he had heard the rumors, and now he was fishing to find out a bit more.

"Yes, I did." She shook her head. "It was horrible. Do you have any idea who might have broken in?" She hoped the change in subject would send a clear message that she didn't want to discuss Martin's death any further. She didn't want to talk about it anymore and worried that her explanation of how she found his body, would only make the rumors worse.

"No, not a clue. But to be honest it seemed to me like whoever it was, was looking for something in particular." He shrugged. "I have no idea what."

"Did you get anything new recently? Anything special?" Charlotte narrowed her eyes. "Maybe the person just couldn't find it?"

"Nothing new at all. You know, a few fruitcakes for Christmas, just the normal Christmas things. Nothing valuable."

"Doesn't sound like anything to break in over. Hmm. What about any servicemen? Did you have anyone in to fix anything recently?" She shifted from one foot to the other and attempted to casually glance over his shoulder into the house.

"No, no one. Oh wait, the cable guy last week. But I don't think he would break in." He shrugged. "Honestly, Charlotte there's no reason for anyone to break into my house."

"What about any recent house guests?" She sensed that he was about to end their conversation.

"Charlotte, you seem very interested in this." He folded his arms across his chest. "Why is that?"

"I think you know why." She cleared her throat. "Blue River means a lot to me. It's my home. I want to make sure that it's safe. The police are very good at their jobs, but sometimes it takes the locals banding together to help solve a crime."

"Sometimes it does." He nodded, then slipped his hands into his pockets. "The only company I've had is a friend of mine, Victoria. She and I have been having dinner now and then. We had dinner earlier this week. I cooked." His lips spread into a proud smile. "I used to be a chef."

"Oh, lucky Victoria." Charlotte tried to hide her reaction with a smile in return. Victoria, who might have killed Martin, had spent time at Benjamin's house? "When exactly did you two have dinner?"

"Uh, it was last night. We had a late dinner, around nine." He cleared his throat. "But she wouldn't have done this. She could come see me at any time, why would she break in?"

"You're right, she wouldn't." Charlotte waved her hand. "I'm sure you two enjoyed your dinner."

"We did." He smiled again, so wide that he

revealed some dimples in his cheeks. "We always do."

"Ah, I see this is a love connection, hmm?" She winked at him.

"Maybe. I never thought it would be possible at my age. But, here I am again." He shrugged.

"I'm happy for you, Benjamin." She offered her hand to him. "I mean that."

"Thanks, Charlotte." He shook her hand, then glanced over his shoulder. "If I figure anything out, I'll let you know. But like I said, I can't think of any reason why anyone would want to break in. I sure hope the police figure it out soon so that we can get back to our peaceful lifestyle."

"Me too." Charlotte nodded to him as he stepped back inside. When she returned to her car, her mind buzzed with the new information. Victoria was having dinner with Benjamin, obviously they had a thing going. But how could that lead to her breaking into his house? Was it possible that she left some evidence of the murder behind? Maybe she thought breaking in was the best way to get it back? If that were the case, why would she break into Mary's house? She decided that she would be sure to ask Mary whether she knew Victoria. She presumed she did, but she wanted to know more details about it.

Going to the class would give her some insight into whether there had been other break-ins or if there might be a deeper connection between them.

~

*A*lly wiped down the counters after another rush had finally died down. As happy as she was that there was so much business, she was also exhausted.

"You weren't kidding about needing help, Ally. I don't know how you keep up with this." Nina leaned against the counter, her cheeks pink from exertion, and her forehead glistening with sweat. "If one more person walks in here and asks for three boxes of candies to go, I think I'm going to lose my mind."

"It's not usually like this." Ally sighed as she stretched her arms above her head in an attempt to loosen up her muscles. "Things are crazy during the holidays, but it seems even busier this year."

"Maybe it's those beautiful boxes of candies that Diana has been handing out. They are so delicious. I bet some people went through the whole box and decided they need more." She began to tidy up the area near the front door.

"I didn't know you knew Diana." Ally studied her. She still wasn't ready to forgive, but it was hard to stay angry at her friend. She was generally a kind person, and even though Ally would have preferred her loyalty, she also knew that deep down her grandmother was right. Nina had a right to her own opinion.

"Yes, she's in my seniors' class. She's quite flexible and dedicated to the class. I really enjoy talking with her about her experiences in life. I guess I was on her Christmas list." She shrugged. "Trust me, I was happy to get the candies."

"I'm glad you enjoyed them." Ally bit down into her bottom lip. She was tempted to apologize again, but she just couldn't. The thought that Nina suspected her grandmother even the slightest bothered her. "Listen, I'm going to close up. I can handle things from here. You go on and have a good night, all right?"

"Sure." She paused as she picked up a cloth. "Ally, I know I overstepped. I hope our friendship won't suffer because of it. I just hate to see anyone harmed in any way. It makes me crazy. I don't always think things through, I just react in a protective way."

"It's all right." Ally walked over to the register to

start to close it down. "You're entitled to your opinion. I can tell you that Mee-Maw had nothing to do with this, but that won't matter unless you believe it. It's not easy for me to think of you suspecting her, but I suppose I can't blame you since the police are also looking at her as a suspect, but that doesn't mean I have to like it."

"I understand." She walked towards the door. "I really appreciate you giving me this opportunity. Thanks, Ally."

Ally glanced up from the register as the door swung shut behind Nina. She was tempted to say more to defend her grandmother, but she knew it would fall on deaf ears. As long as the rumors kept circulating, Charlotte would encounter people who wanted nothing to do with her.

Ally was in the process of shutting down the register when the door swung open. She'd forgotten to lock it after Nina left.

"I'm sorry, but we're closed." She looked up to see Victoria just inside the door. Something about the way the woman gazed at her made her blood run cold.

"I'm not here to buy anything." She stalked towards the counter. "Where's Charlotte?"

"She's not here." Ally stopped short of telling her

about the gift making class. With the way Victoria looked, she didn't want her anywhere near her grandmother.

"Then you can give her a message from me." She locked her eyes to Ally's. "She needs to stay away from Benjamin. I know she's trying to pin this murder on me. I had nothing to do with it. If she keeps tarnishing my reputation, I will make sure that hers doesn't survive. She had plenty of motive, since I happen to know that Jeff was having an affair with Trudy. I've kept it to myself, because I'm not one to spread ugly rumors. But if she shows up at Benjamin's door again, asking him questions about me, I will make sure that everyone in this town knows exactly what kind of jealous woman she is. Maybe she wanted to teach Trudy a lesson. Since she messed with Jeff, Charlotte killed Martin. It seems like a stupid way to get revenge to me, but then again, I'm not a murderer." She swung her hand through the air so sharply that Ally ducked back.

"My grandmother didn't kill anyone!" Ally glared at her. "She would never harm anyone, especially not Martin who she considered to be her friend. There's no way Jeff would betray her, and even if he did, she wouldn't seek revenge for it. The fact that you're here threatening her makes it pretty clear to me that you're trying to hide your own guilt."

"Ha! You'd like that wouldn't you?" She slapped her hand down on the counter. "Too bad I have an alibi, go ahead and ask your badge-wearing boyfriend about it. He'll tell you that I'm off the suspect list. Oops, I guess he isn't keeping you up to date, is he? Maybe he has more important things to focus on while he's away? Charlotte is with a cheater, maybe you are, too!"

Ally opened her mouth to say more, but Victoria turned on her heel and stalked out the door. She hurried behind the woman to lock the door and turn the sign to closed. The entire experience left her rattled. Was it possible that Jeff had been having an affair with Trudy? Was it possible that Victoria wasn't the killer? She decided to call Luke, as Victoria had instructed. If he knew something about Victoria's alibi, she wanted to know what it was. When she dialed his number she couldn't help but wonder what he was doing at that moment. The classes would be over for the day. Was he out at the bar with other cops? Was he alone in his hotel room?

"Hi, sweetheart." His voice sounded tired, heavy with a mixture of emotions.

"Hi, Luke. I'm sorry if I'm interrupting."

"No, I'm just sitting here waiting to hear about possible flights home. The weather is getting crazy. I'm not sure if I'm going to be able to make it."

"Oh." She did her best not to sound disappointed.

"I'm sorry, Ally, I'm still trying."

"It's okay, I understand. Listen, I'm calling to see if you know anything about Victoria having an alibi for the night of Martin's murder." She finished up the closing procedures as she listened to Luke.

"Uh, yeah, I was going to let you know about that. Victoria was visiting her sister the night that Martin was killed. The sister has backed up her alibi."

"But it's her sister, she could be lying to protect her." Ally frowned and finished putting away the last of the chocolates.

"It's possible, but they were able to confirm with the service station where she filled up her car. Her sister lives close to two hours away. She claims Victoria was there until early evening. However, it's possible that Victoria drove back and made it just barely in time to kill Martin. The detective working the case feels it's too much of a stretch to focus on. He's also curious about the break-ins. He thinks it's strange that only the kitchen was rummaged through. And well, he has his sights set on someone different. Victoria told the police that she is certain that Jeff was having an affair with Trudy. I wasn't sure if I should tell you." His voice grew thick. "I'm sorry, Ally."

"I don't believe it." Ally narrowed her eyes. "Jeff just doesn't seem like he would do something like that. But I can tell you I'm going to find out."

"Ally, you need to be careful."

"I know. Thanks for the information, Luke." She started to hang up the phone.

"Ally, wait."

"Yes?" She tried to hold back her frustration.

"I miss you, and I'll see you soon."

"I miss you, too." She sighed as she hung up. She'd almost ended the conversation without saying good-bye properly. That was harsh. But even though she understood why, she was still frustrated that he hadn't come to her right away with the information about Victoria, and especially about Jeff. As she left the shop, she decided that she needed to find out the truth about Jeff right away.

CHAPTER 10

After speaking to Benjamin, Charlotte's mind raced. Now that she knew Victoria was even more strongly connected to one of the victims of the break-ins she was tempted to believe that she had something to do with the murder. But could a battle over Christmas music really lead to killing? She doubted it. She hoped that she would find out something more at the gift making class. Maybe Mary would have more to say than Benjamin did, if she was there. When she stepped into the bustling class, she was a little intimidated. Normally it was a bit quieter, but tonight it seemed everyone in the room was caught up in a conversation. It was easy to assume why with the scandals that were racing through town. Now, not only was Martin dead, but someone was breaking into apartments, and supposedly Charlotte was a murder suspect.

Charlotte hated the way that everyone stared at her when she walked in, but she pretended it didn't bother her. It did. These were her friends, weren't they? Didn't they think it was crazy to even consider that she could kill someone? She forced down her emotions as she spotted the woman she'd come to see. Mary was seated towards the back of the class. She was the only one not engaged in a conversation. Instead, she gazed down at her phone. Maybe she was playing a game, or texting. Charlotte walked up beside her and gave her a light tap on the shoulder. The woman jumped at the sensation, and looked up with wide eyes.

"Sorry, I didn't mean to scare you, Mary."

"That's okay, I'm just a little jumpy."

"I'm glad you came tonight. I wasn't sure if you would." Charlotte sat down beside her.

"I just thought it would be good to be around friends." She frowned as she tucked her phone away. "I'm still feeling a little nervous about going back to my apartment. I've been staying with my friend, Thea."

"I'm so sorry that you went through that. I've always felt so safe living here, it seems odd that all of these break-ins have started. I guess, it's not too unusual around the holiday season, though. Maybe the burglars are looking for gifts or extra cash laying around." She slid over in her chair to be closer to her. "I'm sorry, I shouldn't be debating the whys and hows when all that matters is that something awful has happened."

"No, you're right, at least if there was an explanation for it, I could process it better. But the fact that from what I can tell the intruder didn't take anything, they just searched through my kitchen, is so very strange. Don't you think?" She held her hands up in front of her. "What were they looking for? A pie?" She rolled her eyes.

"Just your kitchen?" Charlotte's mind began to race. Both of the break-ins only involved a search of the kitchen? What did that mean? Were they looking for food, or an appliance? "Yes, that's very strange. What did the police have to say about all of it?"

"The police." She pursed her lips. "Not much, they just took the report and assured me they'd look into it. But I doubt they will. They have their hands full with the murder." She tightened her lips as if the word repulsed her. Charlotte understood, as the mention of it unsettled her, too. "I know I should be calmer, after all nothing valuable was taken, and I wasn't hurt, but it's hard not to feel nervous. What if whoever it was comes back? What if they were just checking to see how easy it was to break in?" She shuddered at the thought. "I'm having an alarm system installed. I've never had one in my life, but now I can't imagine going to sleep in that apartment without one."

"I'm glad you're taking that step." Charlotte nodded. "It can make such a big difference. I was wondering if you've seen Victoria here?" She asked casually as she looked around the room.

"No, I haven't seen her for a few days." She shook her head.

"Are you friendly with her?"

"Not really, we used to be part of the same book club, though. But that was a long time ago."

"Oh okay, I wonder, have you had anything special delivered to your house? Or maybe someone who came to visit that doesn't usually visit?" She met the woman's eyes.

"Uh, no. Not really. Andy and Diana dropped off one of her gifts, but that was it." She shrugged. "The chocolates are delicious by the way." She smiled. "I ate them all the first night, I'm such a pig." She laughed.

"You're not a pig. I'm glad you liked them. I eat quite a few myself." Charlotte grinned. "I don't think I know an Andy."

"Oh, he lives in Freely Lakes, too. The guy with very blond hair, he has a motorcycle that he rides everywhere."

"Oh yes." Charlotte nodded. "The man that lives next to Bob."

"That's him." Mary nodded. "He and Diana are friends. I think he was just helping to tote her boxes around to deliver them."

Charlotte looked up and scanned the room. She didn't see any sign of Diana. That surprised her. Before she could wonder too much about it, Beth walked to the front of the room. She looked distressed as she faced her students.

"I'm sorry, everyone, but I am canceling the class. I just can't continue. I'm very sorry."

An uproar began all around Charlotte. People asked about refunds, others asked about finishing their projects, but Beth turned and hurried out of the classroom without answering any of their questions.

"Oh dear." Mary frowned.

Charlotte followed Beth out of the classroom. The woman practically ran down the hall and around the corner. Charlotte chased after her. When she finally caught up she spotted her as she ducked into a bathroom. She pushed the door open behind her.

"Beth?"

She could hear quiet crying in one of the stalls.

"Beth, if there's anything I can do please just tell me."

"There's nothing, Charlotte, please just leave me alone."

"Beth." She paused in front of the stall. "Maybe if you tell me what's wrong, I can help."

"What's wrong? What's wrong is that everyone is looking at me! A reporter from Mainbry found out about my past with Martin, and published an article on the internet. I'm sure it'll be in the papers by tomorrow morning. It's all about how Martin took all of my money and how I've been holding a grudge. Now, I'm sure that everyone will think I killed Martin!"

"Oh, Beth, I'm so sorry." She narrowed her eyes as she thought about reporters. Some of them made up or embellished things for the sake of a story, but perhaps they had stumbled on to something. She was certainly eager to read the article.

"Yes, he lost my entire investment, and there

were many years that we wouldn't say one word to each other. But life goes on, you know? I just accepted the loss and eventually moved forward. I would never kill anyone over it. But of course, I don't have an alibi. I'm just waiting for the police to come and arrest me. Charlotte, you have no idea how nerve racking it is."

"Yes, I kind of do." Charlotte sighed. "I'm a suspect, too, Beth. It's not easy to face the judgment or the fear of being arrested, but the important thing is that you know you're innocent. I still believe that innocent people are not arrested for crimes they didn't commit."

"If only they could find Trudy. I'm sure she's the one who did it. If the police could get their hands on her, this would all be resolved."

"What makes you think Trudy did it?" She leaned a little closer to the stall door.

"Everyone knows she was having an affair. She probably killed Martin so that she could be with him." She stopped short with a small gasp.

"Him?" Charlotte's heartbeat quickened. "Do you know who he is? Maybe he had something to do with this."

"I shouldn't say. It's just a rumor."

"Please, I'd like to know, Beth. I'm at risk here,

too." She pressed her hand against the stall door, and found that it swung open. Beth hovered near the back of the stall, her eyes filled with tears.

"You really don't know, do you?" She met Charlotte's eyes.

"Know what?" A shiver carried through her, as if she should know.

"It's Jeff."

"Jeff?" Her mouth grew dry. "That's impossible."

"I'm sorry, Charlotte, sometimes people just aren't who we think they are."

Charlotte stared at her for a moment. She knew there were hundreds of questions she should ask, but she couldn't form a single word. Instead she turned and left the bathroom.

~

*I*t only took a few texts for Ally to get Jeff to meet her at his apartment. She didn't want to call, because she was afraid he would hear the suspicion in her voice. On the drive to Freely Lakes she went through an assortment of emotions. Mostly, she was angry. Angry at the thought that

Jeff could hurt her grandmother and angry that he might be allowing her to take the fall for him or Trudy. Maybe he was the one feeding information to the chief about her grandmother. The thought made her stomach lurch with disgust. She knew that Charlotte trusted him, and she usually had good instincts about people. The very thought of having to reveal the news to her grandmother filled her with dread. When she reached Freely Lakes, she looked at her watch. She was relieved to see that the gift making class was still on and her grandmother would still be there, so she would have a little time to speak to Jeff alone. She marched right up to his apartment and knocked loudly on his door. He opened it.

"Ally, now what's all of this about?" He frowned as he gestured for her to step in.

"No thanks, out here is fine." She crossed her arms as she stared at him. "It took me quite some time to be sure that you were good for Mee-Maw, Jeff, and honestly you fooled me. You really did. I thought you were always looking out for her best interests, and that you truly cared for her. But clearly that wasn't true." She narrowed her eyes.

"What?" He leaned against the door frame and stared back at her. "What are you talking about,

Ally?" He spoke so carefully that she guessed he was trying to hide some of his emotions.

"I'm talking about your affair with Trudy. How come everyone in Blue River knows about it, except for me, and Mee-Maw?" She searched his eyes. A small part of her still hoped that he would tell her it wasn't true, that she would be able to believe him, and spare her grandmother the pain that came along with such a betrayal.

"An affair with Trudy?" His cheeks grew red. "Ally, you've got your information wrong."

"Does she?" Charlotte stepped up behind her.

"Mee-Maw, I'm sorry —"

"It's all right, Ally." She placed her hand on her granddaughter's shoulder, then looked straight at Jeff. "It seems there are quite a few rumors buzzing around Blue River right now. One of them is that I'm a killer. That certainly isn't true. So, let's not assume that these rumors about Trudy and Jeff are true. Remember how upset you were with Nina for doubting me?" She glanced over at Ally.

"Yes." Ally bit into her bottom lip. She was amazed that her grandmother could be so calm in the face of such an accusation, and yet she had a point. Nina had assumed the suspicions about her grandmother were true, and it made Ally angry enough to want to fire her.

"Jeff, in case you haven't heard, apparently some people believe that you and Trudy were having an affair. Now, I know that you told me you and Trudy are friends. So, I'm not here to accuse you of anything. I appreciate your honesty. And your personal business is yours. But, you need to be aware that this rumor could lead to you being as much a suspect as I am. So, if there is any truth to it, I suggest you find a way to protect yourself." She started to turn away.

"Charlotte, wait!" He caught her hand and turned her back towards him. "You don't believe any of this, do you?" His eyes drooped as he stared at her. "You don't think I would do anything like this, do you?"

"Kill Martin?" She smiled. "No, not for a second."

"That's not what I meant." He lowered his voice. "I would never cheat on you, Charlotte."

"Never mind that." She waved her hand. "The important thing here is to figure out who killed Martin."

"Yes, that's important, but so is your trust in

me." He continued to gaze into her eyes. "I didn't, and will never, cheat on you."

"There's nothing to cheat on. We're friends, right?" She patted his hand, which still held hers. "Jeff, I know who you are. Nothing can change that."

Ally watched in amazement as she pulled him into a warm hug. "But be careful. Because I don't think I could handle it if you ended up arrested for Martin's murder."

"Trudy was teaching me how to knit." His cheeks burned bright red. "All right? I wanted to make something special for my new granddaughter, and she suggested I knit her a blanket. I mentioned I didn't know how to knit, and she offered to teach me. That was all. I was too embarrassed to tell you."

"Why would you be embarrassed about that?" Charlotte smiled.

"Because, it's not exactly a manly thing to do."

"Aw." She patted his hand again and shook her head. "Jeff, you don't need to hide things from me. But you also don't have to tell me every aspect of your life. I trust you."

"Thank you, Charlotte." He smiled. "You are an amazing woman."

"I don't know about that, Jeff, but I do know

that I'm lucky to have you. Keep your head down, and we'll get through all of this."

"I should go." Ally lowered her eyes. "I'm sorry, Jeff."

"Don't be." He smiled at her. "I'm glad you're so quick to protect Charlotte."

"Thank you, Ally." Charlotte kissed her cheek.

As Ally left, she could still hear them talking. It impressed her that her grandmother was so certain of her trust for Jeff. Could she say the same for herself and Luke?

As she walked down the hallway, she saw someone poke their head around the corner in front of her. It took her a second to realize who it was.

"Trudy?" She ran after her around the corner. However, when she reached the next hallway, there was no sign of her. Maybe it was her imagination.

CHAPTER 11

When Ally arrived at the cottage, she closed the door and released a heavy sigh. It was good to be home, even if it worried her to leave her grandmother alone. She knew that Charlotte liked her space, and she had her own way of sorting through things. However, with a killer on the loose, as well as someone breaking into homes, there was a lot to be concerned about. She wondered how things were going between Charlotte and Jeff, and whether her grandmother would be annoyed that she had tried to interfere.

"Peaches, just who I needed to see." She scooped the cat up into her arms and carried her over to the couch. "You're going to help me figure this out, aren't you?"

Peaches rubbed her cheek against Ally's and purred. Arnold lay down by Ally's feet. A wave of relaxation washed over her. All of the muscles that were tense in her body without her even knowing it, eased, and the release created a warm sensation. She closed her eyes, and released another deep sigh. Then her mind began to clear. Yes, the murder and the break-ins were probably connected. It was too much of a coincidence for them to have taken place so close together.

"I think that whoever killed Martin, is looking for something. But what could be found in the kitchen that would drive someone to kill in order to find it? I mean, most valuables are hidden in closets, or safes, or under the bed. Not in the kitchen." She kicked off her shoes and pulled her feet up on the couch. She continued to stroke Peaches' fur. Was it possible the break-ins weren't being committed by the killer at all, but by someone intent on solving the crime? Maybe they thought evidence could be found in the kitchens of one of these people? But why did they take random items from Benjamin's? To cover their tracks? Or did they find what they were looking for? She had no idea who would be bold enough to do that. But after thinking that she caught a glimpse of Trudy, she had to consider her. She also couldn't rule out Beth, as everyone who experienced a break-in was in her class. Maybe she knew more than she'd told anyone, even the police. Maybe she had her own list of suspects and was trying to narrow it down by breaking into their homes. A few minutes later she heard a knock on the door. Before she could reach it, the door swung open.

"Mee-Maw, I didn't think you'd come over so late."

"I hope you don't mind, I just need to work some things through and you're the only person I can do that with." She hugged Ally. "Thanks for looking out for me with Jeff, Ally."

"I'm sorry if I overstepped." She frowned.

"Not at all. You should hear about some of the conversations I've had with Luke." She winked at her.

"Wait, what conversations?" Ally's eyes widened.

"Never mind that. I need to tell you what happened tonight at class." She recounted Beth's break down, and the information that Mary had given her.

"It's funny, I was just thinking that maybe

whoever is breaking in is looking for evidence." Ally raised her eyebrows. "Do you think it's possible?"

"Yes, I think it's definitely possible. But that's not the only thing I found out. Jeff told me that he's heard of two more people in the gift making class that had their homes broken into. That makes four. I really don't think that can be a coincidence, do you?" She met Ally's eyes.

"No, I don't. It seems like a pattern to me. So maybe whoever is breaking in is after something that is related to that class?" She narrowed her eyes as she sat down beside her grandmother on the couch. "But what could it be? And why were they taking worthless, random items?"

"No idea." Charlotte sighed. "I did find out that the rumors were right, Beth has quite a history with Martin. I read the article about Beth and Martin and it practically painted Beth as the perfect suspect, getting revenge for all of the money she lost. I hate to say it, but their past might be connected to his murder. Let's see what we can find out about the business that closed and who lost what."

"Sure, I'll get on that now." Ally grabbed her computer and carried it over to the dining room table. As she settled down in front of it she felt

Peaches push her nose up against her knee. She slid back enough from the table so that the cat could jump up in her lap. Peaches curled up, and her steady purr helped Ally to relax a little. As much as she wanted to know exactly what was going on she knew that she had to find the pieces that would fit together. Just guessing, or rushing to judgment wasn't going to help the situation.

As Ally began to dig into Martin's past she saw the same things she'd seen before. He barely had an online presence and from what she could find there was nothing remarkable about it. She decided to shift gears, and see what she could find out about Beth. As she began to look into her, a photograph popped up. It was part of an article written about a local women's group. Beth stood in the middle of a group of women. She appeared to be in her forties at the time.

Peaches flicked her tail and opened her eyes. As she gazed at the screen, Ally felt her muscles stiffen. A low growl began deep in the cat's belly.

"What is it, Peaches?" Ally looked down at her. Could the cat really be looking at the photograph on the screen? "Mee-Maw, do you know anything about the Blue River Belles?"

Charlotte looked up from the notebook she'd

been making lists in. She was attempting to connect the four victims of the break-ins and Martin in any way that she could.

"Oh wow, I haven't heard that name in a long time. It was a women's small business group. Beth started it, and any woman in Blue River and the surrounding towns that ran a business or was interested in running a business could join it. A lot of the local women joined. I think Diana was in it, too." She tapped her pen on the notebook. "Why do you ask?"

"I'm looking into Beth, and the picture came up. Were you in the group, too?" Ally shooed Peaches down from her lap as the cat continued to growl. She wasn't sure if Peaches' instincts were telling her something, or if she was just in the mood to play. If she was in the mood to play, then it wasn't safe to have her on her lap in front of a computer screen.

"No, I wasn't. It turned into more of a coffee club than anything else. I already had my business up and running, and to be honest, I wasn't very social in those days. I just thought it was a little silly that a bunch of women would sit around and chit chat, and call it a business meeting." She rolled her eyes. "But it was a very popular group, just about everyone that I knew joined."

"Interesting." Ally printed the picture. "I wonder if the women in this group knew about the failed business that Beth and Martin ran?" She typed a new query into the search bar. "I'm not finding out much about it so far."

"Try looking in the Mainbry directory of businesses. There's one kept on the library's website I think. It's hardly ever maintained, except to add new businesses. I don't think they ever delete the old ones. If they shared a business at one time, it'll likely still be listed on there."

"Great idea, thanks Mee-Maw."

Ally navigated to the library's website, and found the list that her grandmother mentioned. It was so long that it took her quite some time to scroll through. Eventually she came to a travel agency.

"M and B Vacations?" She glanced over at her grandmother. "What do you think?"

"That sounds right. M for Martin, and B for Beth." She shrugged. "That should help you get some more information on the business." Charlotte stifled a yawn.

"Mee-Maw, why don't you go on to bed? I won't be far behind you."

"No, I can't just yet, I think I'm on to something." She swept her pen across the notebook paper, then tapped it twice. "I've found a connection between all of the victims of the break-ins and Martin."

"What is it?" Ally stood up and walked over to join her on the couch.

"Trudy." She smiled some. "She is friends with all of the people that were broken into, and obviously she was Martin's wife."

"You think Trudy is doing the break-ins?" Ally's eyes widened. "It's possible. I thought I saw her tonight."

"You did?" Charlotte stood up. "Where?"

"I thought I saw her in the hall as I was leaving Freely Lakes. But I called to her, and chased after her, and she was gone. It could have been anyone, honestly. If she was back in town, why wouldn't we know about it?"

"Maybe because she's doing the break-ins. What I can't figure out is why." Charlotte stared down at the words on the paper. "Even if she did kill Martin, why would she be rummaging through people's kitchens?" She pursed her lips with confusion.

"I was thinking that maybe she killed Martin, and stashed some evidence in one of her friend's apartments?" Ally frowned. "No that wouldn't work, because she would know which friend."

"Maybe she thinks she knows who killed Martin and is trying to find the proof that she didn't do it?" Charlotte tilted her head from side to side. "That might fit."

"It might." Ally nodded. "If that was Trudy in the hall."

Charlotte covered another yawn. "I guess it is time to turn in."

Ally nodded and made sure her grandmother had everything she needed in her old bedroom which she kept furnished for whenever she wanted to sleep over. Arnold followed after Charlotte and snuggled up next to her on the bed. Ally went to her own room and went straight to bed. Within minutes Peaches was curled up on her belly.

CHAPTER 12

When Charlotte woke up the next morning she discovered that Ally had already left for the shop, and left behind a note.

Nina will be in early, so please take some time off.

Charlotte considered the note for a moment. She knew that Ally could certainly use some help at the shop. But she also knew that a little free time might help her investigate the murder. Now that she knew that the police might be looking at Jeff as a suspect, she had even more reason to solve the crime as soon as possible. The moment she thought of him, her cell phone rang.

"Can you meet me for breakfast?" His rushed tone indicated that he had a pressing reason for the meeting.

"Sure, I can. When?"

"As soon as you can. I'm heading to the diner now."

"All right, I'll head out now." She reached down and patted Arnold's nose as he snorted at her leg. "I'll be back in a little bit, buddy."

As she headed out the door she wondered what Jeff might be upset about. Was he still worried that she doubted him? Or had the police been out to visit him that morning?

It took only a few minutes to reach the diner. Once she was there she parked and hurried towards the door. However, a familiar face made her stop in her tracks.

"Trudy?" Charlotte paused in front of the diner and stared hard at the woman.

"Yes?" She smiled at Charlotte. "It's good to see you."

"Trudy, you've been gone —"

"Oh, I know. I've been staying with my friend. You know Julie." She rolled her eyes. "I needed to let Martin cool down a bit. He was so up in arms over the Christmas decorations, and honestly I just couldn't take it anymore. I think if I'd heard him say one more thing about garland, or bulbs, I would have killed him." She laughed. "I was just going to grab something to eat before I headed home, to face the Christmas music." She laughed again.

"Oh dear." Charlotte's heart sunk as she gazed at the woman. "You haven't been told, have you?"

"Been told what?" Trudy's cheerful expression grew slack, as if she anticipated bad news. "Charlotte, is something wrong?"

Charlotte had no idea how to tell her, or even if she should tell her, but she knew that Trudy would hear about it the moment that she stepped into the diner. There was no way to hide it from her, and though breaking the news would be hard, she would at least be delicate about it, while others might not be.

"Come sit here with me, Trudy." She gestured to a bench in front of the restaurant. "I need to tell you something." Her eyes moistened as she recalled the moment she'd seen Martin on the ground. Perhaps she would have found Trudy as well if she had been there. Of course, she might have been. She might have been the only one who knew exactly what happened because she killed her husband. She pushed away the thought. Yes, Trudy was a suspect, and yes it seemed as if she might have had a motive, but that didn't mean that she was guilty. Charlotte had the unexpected duty of revealing the truth about her husband's death, and if she was innocent of the crime, that would be a huge shock. Once Trudy sat down beside her, Charlotte took her hand and looked into her eyes.

"Trudy, the police have been looking for you. Martin has been killed." She thought it best to plunge right into it, as no beating around the bush would change the truth. "I'm so sorry for your loss."

"What?" She tugged her hand free of Charlotte's. "That's not a funny joke. Why would you even say something like that?" Her cheeks reddened.

"It's not a joke, Trudy. I'm so sorry to tell you this, but he's gone. He was killed the night you left, and the police have been looking for you ever since. I suggest that you hire a lawyer, and then go into the station."

"What?" Her mouth hung open as the word echoed through the air. "This can't be happening. It can't be true." She began to rock back and forth on the bench.

"It is. I found him myself. I don't think he suffered." She took her hand again and gave it a supportive squeeze. "I'm here for you, Trudy. I can't imagine how it must feel to get this kind of news. But you're not alone, I'm right here with you."

"Thank you, Charlotte," she stammered out her words as tears began to roll down her cheeks. "Who did it? Who killed him?" She paused, as if finally fitting a few things together. "Oh, my goodness, they think I did it? Is that why I need a lawyer? We had a fight, and then—" Her words were swallowed up by a sob.

"Listen, a spouse is always a suspect until they're not. All you have to do is talk to the detective, give him your alibi, and things will get wrapped up. He'll be able to tell you more about what happened." Charlotte frowned as she rubbed her hand along the back of Trudy's palm. "I'm so sorry, hon. I know how much you two loved each other."

"But we didn't." She sniffled. "We didn't really."

"What?" Charlotte blinked. "What are you saying?"

"We hadn't loved each other in a long time. I stayed with him because I couldn't afford to live apart from him. He had all of the money, he was so stingy." She shuddered. "I should go. I should get to the police station. Charlotte, do you think they will arrest me?" Fresh tears spilled down her cheeks. "Oh, the very thought of those handcuffs on me. Do you know what they make you do when you get arrested?"

"It's all right," Charlotte said with determination. She refused to believe that the truth wouldn't be revealed. "They have to have enough evidence to arrest you, and I'm sure they don't. They can't. Because you're innocent."

"Yes, of course I am. But it doesn't look good, does it? We have a fight, I disappear, and then he's killed?" Her voice cracked on her final word. "Oh, poor Martin. No, he wasn't a good man, but he wasn't the worst either. He didn't deserve this. Who would do this to him?"

"I don't know. Can you think of anyone? Had he been arguing with anyone lately? Or maybe someone from his past?" Charlotte tried to analyze the woman's expression.

"I, I don't know. He always had problems with Victoria of course. But I'm sure she wouldn't kill him." She sighed and rubbed her hands across her face. "How can this be happening? How can I be trying to figure out who killed my husband?"

"I'm sorry, Trudy. If there's anything I can do, please don't hesitate to call me." She pressed a business card into her hand. "I'm here to help."

"Thanks, Charlotte." She stared into her eyes for a moment, then stood up and wandered off into the parking lot. Charlotte was tempted to follow her, but she knew the woman was too upset to tell her much more. Or at least she appeared to be.

As Charlotte stepped into the diner, she noticed that Jeff was already seated at one of the tables. She headed over to him, with her mind still spinning. Had he been meeting Trudy? She did trust him, but she couldn't help but wonder. As she sat down at the table, he leaned close to her.

"You're not going to believe this." He sounded a bit out of breath.

"What is it?" She searched his eyes as she noticed the concern in his expression.

"My apartment was broken into this morning. I went for a short walk and when I came back it had been broken into. Nothing is missing that I know of, but the place was turned upside down." He slipped his hand into hers. "Charlotte, if it can happen to me, it can happen to you, I don't want you staying in your apartment alone."

"Jeff, I'm sorry this happened." She smiled slightly. "I'm not scared, but if it will put your mind at ease I'm sure I can stay with Ally tonight, she won't mind, and I can spend some time with her. But what about you?" She leaned back and looked into his eyes again.

"I doubt anyone is going to break in again." His

cheeks flushed. "I can't believe I didn't take more precautions when I heard about the break-ins. If I had put a camera up then, we would have already caught whoever is doing this! I feel so foolish."

"You couldn't have predicted that anyone would break into your home." She narrowed her eyes. "It's strange, because so far only people in the gift making class have been targeted and only their kitchens searched."

"It's strange, that's for sure. Maybe they found what they were looking for in the other apartments so they stopped searching." He wiped his hand across his forehead. "When I reported it to the police, they acted like it was just another case to study instead of someone who needed help."

"I'm sorry about that." She decided to tell him about running into Trudy. "Trudy is back. I just saw her outside. Did you talk to her?"

"She's back? No, I didn't see her." He sighed.

"She didn't even know about Martin."

"You had to break the news?"

"Unfortunately."

"Did she have anything important to say."

"No, I think she's still in shock."

"Well, I hope she can shed some light on all of this."

"Me too." Charlotte smiled, but she already knew that she probably wouldn't. If the crime was going to be solved, it was going to take more than just asking a few questions.

"I'm going to be a little late to the party tonight, but I will be there."

"Party?" She blinked, then nodded. "I almost forgot."

"We should try to be a bit festive."

"Yes, we should!" Charlotte smiled with determination.

CHAPTER 13

*A*lly drove home from the shop, exhausted, but determined to head back within an hour to get more orders done. For the first time she understood her grandmother's dedication to the shop. Sure, most of the time it wasn't very difficult work, but there were times when it demanded blood, sweat, and tears. Those were the times when she was relieved that she loved working in the shop. When she arrived at home, she smiled at the sight of her car in the driveway. Her grandmother was using it while Ally used the van from the chocolate shop. When she opened the door she found Charlotte feeding the animals.

"Oh thanks, Mee-Maw, I'm so late. They are probably ready to make an escape plan." She rolled her eyes.

"Don't worry about it. They are tougher than you think." She tilted her head towards Peaches. "This one played dead until I opened the can of cat food, then she was scampering everywhere."

"Naughty Peaches." She laughed.

"I have so much to tell you." Charlotte leaned against the counter and filled Ally in on seeing Trudy, and Jeff having his apartment broken into, while Ally threw some leftovers on a plate.

"So how did Trudy seem? Do you think it might be her?"

"I don't know. She seemed shocked, to be honest."

"Hmm." Ally pulled the plate out of the microwave. "And now Jeff was broken into? That's odd."

"Yes, it is. Don't forget, we have a party to attend." Charlotte flopped down on Ally's couch.

"No, you have a party to attend." Ally pinned her brown hair up on the top of her head. "I've got to get back to the shop and take care of some orders that backed up today. I got caught up talking to Mrs. Cale, Mrs. White, and Mrs. Bing, and missed a few calls. Then I forgot to check the messages until closing. Luckily, Nina has agreed to meet me there to help out."

"Are you sure? I could come and help." Charlotte studied her. "You're wearing yourself out, Ally."

"I'm fine, really, Mee-Maw. I want you to go to the party. You might be able to find out more information. Plus, I might pick Nina's brain a bit. I think she knows more about all of this than she's saying."

"Why is that?" Charlotte raised an eyebrow.

"Something she said to Mrs. White today. She said the crime would be easy to solve if the investigators looked close to home. That the murderer is often the obvious suspect." She shook her head. "I know she reads a lot of mystery novels, but it just felt like she meant something else by it. You know?"

"Yes." She nodded. "I hear you. I'll see what I can find out tonight. It just seems a little strange to go to a Christmas party after what happened to Martin."

"Mee-Maw, I know this must be hard for you." Ally sat down beside her. "But I don't think Martin would have wanted you to miss out on your favorite party of the year." She rubbed her grandmother's back as she continued to speak. "Maybe being around friends, music, and good food, will help you relax."

"I'm sure it would." She folded her hands in her

lap. "And you're right, Martin wouldn't want me to miss it. He loved Christmas. But the main reason I'm going is to find out more information."

"Exactly. We're stuck right now. Victoria seems to have an alibi. We can't prove that it was Trudy, and even Beth seems like a flimsy suspect. Maybe all of the interaction will shake something loose that we haven't thought of."

"Maybe." Charlotte nodded as she gave Ally's hand a squeeze. "All right, I'll find something to wear. I'm so lucky to have you."

"The feeling is mutual." She kissed her grand-mother's cheek just before she stood up. "Listen, I didn't mention it earlier as I was hoping it might all get worked out, but it looks like Luke might not make it back for Christmas."

"Oh no, Ally, I'm so sorry." She frowned.

"It's all right, the important thing for me is that he's safe. We'll still have a wonderful dinner."

"Yes, we will." Charlotte gave her one more hug. "I'd better get going if I'm going to change."

"If you need anything, just call me. Jeff will be with you, right?"

"Yes, he's supposed to be meeting me there."

"Good." Ally took a deep breath. "Then I'm going to stuff this in my belly, and head back to the shop. Have fun, Mee-Maw." She waved to her as she left the cottage.

As Ally ate she was joined by Peaches on the couch. "Playing dead for treats, hmm?" She winked at her as she fed her a small piece of her chicken. "I know, I know, it doesn't feel much like Christmas, does it?" She closed her eyes and thought about all of the wonderful holidays she'd spent at the cottage. The majority of her happiest moments happened under this roof. She could only hope that she could create another happy moment when she held Christmas dinner there. She smiled as her phone rang. It was Luke.

"Hey, sweetie."

"Hi, I wanted to check in and make sure that Jeff was still alive."

"He is." She laughed. "Actually, Mee-Maw trusted him. He claims they were getting together to knit. A little odd, yes, but if Mee-Maw believes him, I believe him, too."

"Interesting. I'm glad that you took it easy on him. I hope you'll do the same for me. I still haven't been able to get a ticket home."

"Don't worry. We will have lots of holidays to spend together. Just promise me you'll stay warm." She patted Arnold's back as he wiggled past her.

"I promise. Though nothing could be as warm as your arms, and that fireplace."

"Soon enough you'll be home."

As she hung up the phone, she did experience that warm familiar feeling. She'd love for him to be home for Christmas, but the truth was if the murder didn't get solved, he'd return home to a ton of work.

~

As Charlotte stepped into the recreation center, she was surprised by how it had been transformed in such a short time. It felt a bit like walking into a winter wonderland with all of the white fluff and silver tinsel. Near the door, she spotted Beth. She looked transformed as well, in a dark green dress lined at the cuffs and the hem with white faux fur.

"The decorations are exquisite." Charlotte smiled as she swept her gaze over the holly, garland, and sparkling lights. "It's magical."

"Thanks." Beth smiled. "I wanted to use everything I've learned about decorating over the past year. Honestly, it didn't cost very much to put together. It was a bit of work, though."

"I imagine it was. Did you have any help?" She

followed her towards a small table near the back wall.

"Not really. Everyone is so skittish over Martin's death that no one wanted to leave their apartments to help out. But it all got done, and that's the important thing, right?" She shrugged.

"Right." Charlotte studied her for a few moments. "How are you holding up with all of this?"

"Better than I should be, I suppose. I just keep thinking about how Martin and I were once friends. It hurts me to think that all of our bad history is being brought up again. I heard that Trudy was back, so hopefully all of this will get settled soon." She pursed her lips.

"Do you really believe that Trudy would kill him?" Charlotte studied her expression.

"I think it's possible, yes. You didn't know them the way I did. Martin was so focused on money. That was the problem with our business. He wanted my money, not my opinion. He liked to be in control of everything. You'd think that Trudy would have been a third partner, but she wasn't. He wouldn't let her anywhere near the business." She sighed. "He kept their money locked up tight. I'm not sure that Trudy ever even had a dime to spend. He never bought her anything, but every year he would spend so much money on things for himself and new Christmas decorations."

"Wow, I didn't realize that." She frowned. "That must have been very difficult for Trudy. Did she ever fight with him about it?"

"Sometimes." Beth folded her hands together in front of her. Charlotte noticed that she squeezed them tight. "But then she learned not to."

"Learned not to?" Charlotte's heart lurched.

"If they had an argument, he would threaten to leave her, to kick her out on the street with not a penny to her name. He would detail how he could do it. It was terrible." She shivered. "Diana was there, too. It was when she first started renting the apartment from them."

"Wait, what?" Charlotte cleared her throat. "Are you saying that Martin owned Diana's apartment?"

"Sure. He bought it when they first moved into Freely Lakes. He considered it an investment. I actually hooked them up with Diana, as she was in a women's business group with me. Blue River Belles." She rolled her eyes. "That's so long ago now."

"I had no idea."

"Most people don't. It's kind of frowned upon.

Most people expect residents to own their own apartments, but when Freely Lakes first opened they were eager to sell as many apartments as they could. Anyway, I'm not sure what she'll do now. I guess it depends on what happens with Trudy."

"Yes, I guess it does. Excuse me, Beth." Charlotte spotted Diana working her way through the crowd of people. She wanted to speak to her while she had the chance.

As she approached she could hear the conversation Diana was having with Gail.

"Did you like my gift?" She grinned.

"Oh yes I did, I ate all the candies." Gail smiled. "I didn't even save any for my husband."

"Naughty!" Diana laughed, then turned towards Bill. "What about you, Bill, have you opened my gift, yet?"

"I have. I know I should have waited till Christmas, but I couldn't help myself. I have already eaten about half the box. I can't thank you enough for the treat. And the box that you painted is very nice."

"Oh, thank you." She waved to someone on the other side of the room. "Excuse me, I see someone I need to speak to."

As she hurried across the room Charlotte noticed that she pulled out a notebook and made a mark on it before she paused near another woman. "Sheila, have you had a chance to open the gift I dropped off to you?"

"The gift?" She blinked. "Oh yes, now I remember, I opened it, but I haven't had any yet. I'm trying to lose weight before New Year's so I won't have any before next year. But I'm sure they're delicious. I really like the box you made, too."

"Oh wonderful." She smiled. "It took a lot of time to make them. I'm so glad that you liked it."

Charlotte was surprised that she was so blatantly seeking compliments for her gifts. It seemed a bit impolite. But then maybe she was just so excited about the gifts and the holidays that she couldn't resist. She tapped her lightly on the shoulder.

"Diana?"

"Oh!" She jumped as she spun around. "Charlotte, you scared me."

"I'm sorry, I didn't mean to. Do you have a minute to talk?"

"Sure, just a minute though, I have some friends waiting for me to join them." She smiled at Sheila as she walked off.

"I won't keep you, I promise. I just heard that Martin owned your apartment. Do you have any idea what you will do now that he's gone?" She studied her.

"Oh, uh, well. Hopefully Trudy will let me keep renting it. I mean, if she isn't convicted for his murder. Other than that, I'm not really sure." She shrugged. "Time will tell I suppose."

"You're not worried?" Charlotte raised an eyebrow.

"It's Christmas, Charlotte. I'm going to enjoy it, no matter what. Now I have to get going." She started to walk away then turned back. "Did Jeff eat his candies, yet?"

"Oh uh…yes." Charlotte's voice wavered slightly. She couldn't tell her that Jeff had given his gift away.

"He did?" She looked at her with a strange look in her eyes. "I felt a little silly after I realized who I'd given the candies to. I'm sure he gets to have them all of the time."

"He does, but it's always special to get a gift from a friend." Did Diana know Jeff had given her gift away? Is that why she was fishing?

"Yes, it is." She smiled once more, then walked away towards a group of women. Charlotte started to turn away, as she did she found Jeff behind her.

"Charlotte, you are a sight for sore eyes."

"Jeff, I just found out something interesting." She met his eyes.

"Wait." He smiled. "First I just want to dance with you. Okay?"

"Okay." She laughed as he led her on to the dance floor.

CHAPTER 14

*A*lly had the chocolate melting when she heard the door open. She'd left it open for Nina so that she could get started on some of the orders.

"Back here, Nina!" She stirred the chocolate and savored the smell.

"Ally?" Mrs. White made her way into the kitchen.

"Oh! Mrs. White, I thought you were Nina. I'm sorry. We're closed." She was startled by the woman's presence, but not alarmed.

"I know, sweetheart. I probably should have called you, but what I have to say needed to be said in person." She stepped closer to her. "You know, I don't usually gossip."

"What is it, Mrs. White?" Ally locked eyes with her.

"Everyone's at the party tonight. But I just couldn't enjoy it. I've had something on my mind, and I need to tell someone. I'm not certain about it, so I didn't want to go to the police. But I think you should know." She reached out and took Ally's hand. "Please understand that what I'm about to say is only a suspicion."

"I'm listening." Ally ignored the smell of the chocolate as it began to burn.

"Diana came to me last week. She was beside herself with concern. She said that Martin was intent on selling his apartment and hers. She had nowhere to go, and said she couldn't possibly afford to rent another place let alone the cost of moving. I suggested that she try to find a roommate situation, but that only made her more upset. She insisted that Freely Lakes was her home, it was all she had, and that she'd rather die than move. Honestly, I thought I'd talked her through it. I advised her to talk to Martin, to explain everything she'd just told me, and that I was sure he'd be reasonable. This was just a few days before he was killed." She pressed her hand against her stomach. "I asked her today what the plan was for her apartment. She said that she and Trudy had an understanding. Something about the way she said it, just left me unsettled. I don't know, Ally, do you think I'm crazy?"

"I don't think you're crazy, no." Ally smiled. "But as far as I know Diana was with Andy handing out her gifts the night that Martin was killed. I don't think she would have been able to commit the crime."

"Oh, that's a relief!" She sighed. "I'm so sorry I even thought it, to be honest. I do love Diana."

"You should always trust your instincts, Mrs. White." She turned the heat off, and frowned. "I'll make sure I mention it to Luke. It could have been something they overlooked. At this point I think the police will look into any lead they can get. I know their eyes are on Trudy, but I doubt they will find any evidence against her."

"Do they need it?" Mrs. White shook her head. "Sometimes I think a wife is guilty until proven innocent."

"It seems to be that way."

"I'm sorry to interrupt you, Ally. But you should be more careful. I was surprised to find that the door was open." Mrs. White met Ally's eyes with a stern look. "You never know where danger is lurking."

"Yes, you're right. Thank you, Mrs. White." She walked her to the door, and greeted Nina as she stepped in.

"Hi, Nina."

"Hi." She smiled at Mrs. White. "Sorry I'm a little late."

"It's all right. Thanks again, Mrs. White." Ally closed the door behind her and locked it. She didn't think Diana could have anything to do with the murder, but she also didn't want to eliminate any possibilities. Was Diana really handing out chocolates during Martin's murder? She decided she would try to find out. But first, there was chocolate to make.

"What was she doing here?" Nina pulled on an apron. "She looked upset."

"She just had something she wanted to discuss with me." Ally shrugged and led her into the kitchen.

"You can tell me, you know, I won't repeat it." Nina washed up at the sink.

"I just don't know if there is anything to tell. Do you know Diana well? You said she gave you a box of chocolates, right?"

"Yes, like I said she's in one of my classes." She hesitated for a moment. "She's a good woman."

"So, you do know her well?" Ally began to stir a fresh batch of chocolate.

"We're close. I don't know many people here and I don't have much of a connection with my own mother. So, in some ways she's taken over that role for me." She set up some molds for Ally to pour the chocolate into.

"She has some financial trouble, doesn't she?" She glanced over at Nina before she started to pour the chocolate.

"I'm not sure what kind of question that is, but she has the normal struggles. She's a senior woman with no family and no husband. She lives on a fixed income. One stroke of bad luck could cause her to lose everything." She frowned. "It's such a shame that people are forced to live like that."

"Yes, it is." Ally finished pouring the chocolate and started another batch while Nina took care of the molds. Ally watched her out of the corner of her eye. She couldn't help but wonder if Nina was protective of Diana. Maybe she'd heard about Martin trying to sell the apartment. But would she really take it so far as to kill him?

"I'm sorry about suspecting your grandmother, you know? I don't really think she did it. Now that Trudy's back, I'm sure it will all be buttoned up."

"Yes, buttoned up." Ally focused on the chocolate. If Nina did have something to do with Martin's death, she didn't want to give her any reason to suspect that she was on to her.

By the time Ally left the shop for the evening, she was both exhausted and curious. If Nina and Diana were so close, why hadn't Nina made that clear when she'd spoken about her before? It seemed as if she might be hiding something.

When Ally let herself into the cottage, she expected it to be dark. It was late, and she guessed her grandmother would be sleeping. Instead the living room light was on, there was music playing, and Charlotte greeted her at the door with a glass of wine.

"All right, we have some figuring out to do." She waved Arnold out of the way and headed for the couch with her notepad. Together the two reviewed the information they knew about. "From speaking to a few people, including Trudy, I found out that apparently Martin was in control of the finances. Apparently, every penny spent seemed to go towards something that Martin wanted, not anything that Trudy would be interested in. She didn't spend money on herself, isn't that strange?"

"That is very strange. Diana had a lot to lose if

Martin decided to sell her apartment." Ally narrowed her eyes. "If it weren't for her alibi during the crime, I'd think she was definitely a suspect."

"But the alibi hasn't really been confirmed. It isn't foolproof."

"True."

"But I think Beth is still a viable suspect, she has no alibi, and she lost a lot because of Martin." She wrote a few notes on the notepad. "So, we'll want to review things with Beth and Diana. I never thought I'd consider her a suspect, but yes, I do think it's possible. I hate the thought of someone breaking into Jeff's apartment, and of course he breaks the pattern. We thought the break-ins were happening to students of the gift making class, but Jeff isn't one of them."

"No, he isn't. But he is connected to you, and you are one of them." Ally tilted her head back and forth. "Maybe that's the connection." She ran her hand across Peaches' fur.

"Maybe. I guess we'll have to see what we can straighten out tomorrow." Charlotte wiped a hand across her eyes. "I'm pretty wiped out."

"Me, too." Ally stretched her arms into the air.

"You have chocolate in your hair." Charlotte laughed.

"Ugh, I hope that doesn't mean there's hair in the chocolate." Ally grimaced.

"If there is, someone will certainly let you know."

~

Over breakfast the next morning, Charlotte decided what she wanted to do first.

"I'm going to see Trudy again."

"Are you sure you want to do that?" Ally eyed her for a moment. She knew that her grandmother trusted Jeff, but what if she shouldn't? Or what if Trudy thought there was more between herself and Jeff than just friendship? That could lead to an awkward situation. Not to mention they hadn't eliminated Trudy as a suspect. In fact she was still their best one.

"I just want to speak to her one more time. After we had our last conversation, I haven't been able to get something off my mind." Charlotte headed for the door.

"What something?" Ally followed after her.

"Their financial situation, the more I think about it the more certain I am that it means something." She paused at the door. "She said that

Martin and her were having trouble, but she couldn't afford to leave him. Maybe things were strained because he was so tight with his money. Their finances and the fact that Martin spent his money on his Christmas decorations, but not on Trudy, makes me very suspicious. He never even bought her anything. I want to ask her more about that. I wonder if he was withholding money from her, and maybe if she got rid of him she would have access to more money. I mean I don't believe that Trudy would do this, but if he was holding things back financially, then she might have had a good motive to attack him."

"I also think so." Ally frowned.

"Also, if someone feels trapped by someone else for long enough, anything is better than being stuck in that position. I'll let you know what I find out." She headed out the door in a rush. She wanted to get to Trudy before she decided to move out of her friend's house, or she might not know where she ended up next. As she parked alongside Julie's house, she was stunned by the sight of a patrol car parked in the driveway. She swallowed back her apprehension and headed up the driveway to the front door. As she knocked, she could hear voices inside.

"But I didn't do it! I didn't! You can't do this to me!"

Her skin crawled as she realized that was Trudy's voice, more frightened than she'd ever heard it. Another stern voice responded with a command for compliance. Julie opened the door with wide eyes.

"Charlotte, this isn't a good time."

"Don't open that door!" The officer barked at her. Charlotte didn't recognize him. But she did see the way he gripped Trudy's arm. She backed away from the door as she realized things could get out of control very quickly if she wasn't careful. By the time she reached her car, the officer was outside the door. He led Trudy towards the patrol car.

"Charlotte! Charlotte! I didn't kill him! I swear I didn't!" Trudy tugged at the cuffs on her wrists.

"It's all right, Trudy, I don't think you did." She started to move towards her friend, but before she could take a step the officer fixed her with a fierce glare.

"Not another step." He jerked open the rear passenger door and guided Trudy into the car.

Charlotte's stomach flipped with fear and dread. She wanted nothing more than to run to Trudy, to shield her from the horrible experience. But she knew that she couldn't. Clearly, the officer had a warrant for her arrest, which meant the District Attorney's office felt they had enough evidence to make the arrest.

As Charlotte watched the police car roll past, her heart ached for the woman who gazed out at her.

Julie stepped out of the house and walked down the front lawn to join her.

"Can you believe it? I never thought this would happen."

"I can't." Charlotte shook her head, although she did have some doubts of Trudy's innocence she didn't want to voice them. "I don't think Trudy had anything to do with this."

"I guess the evidence will have to speak for itself." Julie crossed her arms as she watched the police car pull away. "As they say, you never truly know someone, no matter how close you think you are." As she turned to walk back into the house, Charlotte stared after her. If Trudy's closest friend was willing to turn her back on her, what did that say about Trudy?

Maybe Charlotte's assumption of Trudy's innocence was wrong. Even though she did have her suspicions due to the information she had found out about Martin controlling Trudy's finances and Trudy disappearing, deep within her she still felt that Trudy had nothing to do with her husband's murder. It didn't matter to her that there were rumors about her and Jeff, or even that Trudy might have hoped for more between them. All that mattered was that she believed an innocent woman was being hauled off to prison, right before her eyes. She had to find out the truth, and fast.

CHAPTER 15

*A*lly set out some fresh samples and tried to keep her mind on the shop. It was hard to concentrate on making cheerful Christmas chocolates when trying to solve a murder was constantly on her mind. The door swung open and in walked Mrs. Bing, Mrs. White, and Mrs. Cale. Ally smiled at them, but to her surprise, none of them smiled in return. One by one they filed up to the counter. Despite the fresh samples, each kept their hands at their sides.

"What's wrong?" Ally stared at them as her apprehension grew. For these three ladies to be so serious, she knew that it had to be something terrible.

"Trudy has been arrested," Mrs. Bing gasped out, then popped a chocolate into her mouth.

"Oh." Ally frowned. "I can't say that surprises me."

"Not me either." Nina added from a few steps away. She set down a fresh tray of chocolates.

"Well, it should." Mrs. Cale fixed them each in turn with a look of disgust. "Trudy would never do this, and I'm surprised at you both, you in particular, Ally, that you're not more upset about this."

"I'm sorry, Mrs. Cale." Ally was surprised by her reproachful stare. "I just meant that the police have been looking for her for so long, I didn't think it would take them long to arrest her. I didn't mean that I think she's guilty."

"Oh, I see." Mrs. Cale nodded. "I suppose I jumped ahead of myself a little there. Trudy is a sweet woman, so soft-spoken. She taught me how to knit. I just hate to think of her locked up."

"It's going to be okay." Mrs. White patted her shoulder. "The truth will come out, either way."

"Do you really think someone will find out the truth and help Trudy?" Mrs. Cale looked directly at Ally.

"Yes, I do." Ally's cheeks flushed. Not long after the three left, Ally looked up to see another familiar face. Her heart skipped a beat when she saw who it was.

"Hi, Diana."

"Hi." She smiled as she walked up to the counter. "My candies were so delicious, and you had the order perfect for me. I'd like another box, just for myself now."

"Sure, let me get that for you. Did you bring one of your boxes in for us to put on display?" She gathered a box of chocolates for her.

"No, sorry. I forgot. Well, to be honest, I used them all. I may have to make another batch of them, but I am a bit worn out creatively right now." She rested her hands against the counter.

Ally noticed that one of her hands had some bruising around the thumb and first finger. "Ouch, what happened?" She handed over the box of chocolates.

"Oh, that's from making the boxes, and carrying them around to hand them out. It's nothing really, I just bruise easily." She rolled her eyes. "Another symptom of being old. Stay young, Ally, for as long as you can."

"Oh, you're still young, Diana. In fact, I admire how independent you are. You live alone, you're very creative, and you always seem to be on the ball with what's happening around town." She smiled as she rung up the chocolates. "I still miss living with Mee-Maw to be honest."

"Oh, do you? Not me. I love my space. I love in particular my apartment. I have everything just the way I want it, and not a soul can change that. No one is there to complain about what I cook, or where I hang things, or when I fold my laundry. It is beautiful." She grinned. "Trust me, one day you'll thank your lucky stars to be on your own."

"You may be right about that." Ally accepted payment from her, and again noticed the bruising on her hand. It looked pretty serious to her. "Did you have a doctor look at that? It's so dark."

"No need, I know my body. Like I said, I bruise easily. I may have underestimated how heavy all of those boxes were."

Ally bit into her bottom lip to keep from pointing out that she knew she had Andy helping her. She remembered the way Mrs. Cale had looked at her, as if she was making it her responsibility to get Trudy out of jail and catch the right killer.

"Maybe something more lightweight next year. You know, I bet Martin really enjoyed his gift, the box was beautiful and he might have even enjoyed the chocolates straight away. I'm sure it was a nice thing for him to receive. It gives me some comfort to think that he had a good memory before he passed." Ally's heart threatened to jump right up into her throat. She knew she was treading on dangerous ground.

"Oh, well, I didn't give him one." Diana cleared her throat. "I was going to give him one closer to Christmas." She nervously turned towards the door.

"So, you were going to give him one?" Ally stepped around the counter. "I know you are friends with Trudy, but I wasn't sure if you were going to give them a gift, because I heard rumors that you and Martin had a falling out." Ally tried to get more information out of her.

"That's not really any of your business, Ally, is it?" She shot her a look of warning. "I have to be going now." She pushed her way through the door.

Ally knew that chasing after Diana wouldn't do her any good. She'd dug a little too deep, and now Diana was defensive. But she'd also gained some insight. Diana seemed very nervous when she mentioned Martin and Trudy. They were her neighbors, who had been her friends for so long, and were also her landlords. Maybe they really did have a falling out.

Ally took a few minutes and quickly searched through Diana's social media. She would have asked her grandmother to do it, but she wasn't as comfortable on the internet as Ally. She wanted to check into whatever she could find out about Diana. She found that Diana was very isolated. Although she had a few friends that posted, there were no signs of family members, or any romantic interests in her life. There were a lot of posts from internet games, and also comments about how it felt to be alone.

Ally did notice that Nina was one of her friends. She'd also shared every post from Nina's yoga studio. It seemed to her that their relationship was pretty strong. She quickly sent a text to her grandmother briefly explaining what she had found out and asking her to see if she could find out if there was anything else interesting about Diana. As another wave of customers entered the shop, Ally glanced over at Nina. She was hard at work boxing up chocolates for orders. She seemed like such a great person, and yet, beneath that soft smile, Ally sensed something hidden.

～

The moment that Ally requested Charlotte find out more information about Diana, Charlotte called her friend Meritza who worked at the courthouse. It was the best place to start to find out information quickly. Maybe Diana was hiding a criminal past. Meritza might have access to court records if there were any. Meritza was happy to help and after a few minutes returned to the phone and said that she had found a petition to purchase her apartment from Martin. It was a year old and had been denied. After thanking Meritza and promising to bring by some chocolates she hung up.

"It must have been very frustrating for Diana to be denied the opportunity to buy her own home," Charlotte mumbled to herself.

She recalled Mary saying that Andy had helped her deliver the chocolates. Andy was new to town and she had never been introduced to him formally. She hoped he didn't know that she owned the chocolate shop or her plan might not work. She decided to swing by his apartment on her way out to the shop. When she knocked on the door, he answered right away.

"Can I help you?"

Charlotte smiled at him. She didn't know him well enough for much small talk.

"Hi, I heard you were delivering chocolates, and I was just wondering if you had any more?" She raised an eyebrow.

"Oh, can't get enough, huh?" He laughed. "Well, I don't know who told you what, but I was just helping out a friend. Diana is the one who was giving away the chocolates. You're going to have to ask her."

"Oh! Okay, thanks. But I still wonder how I missed her delivery. Do you know about what time you started out?" She glanced away casually and hoped that he wouldn't find the question strange.

"Oh, it was a bit before eight. I remember because I was going to watch a show that night, and I thought I would stop and drop off something that I had borrowed from her quickly. I recorded the show just in case I was late." He shrugged. "It was a bit late for delivering gifts, but when I got there she seemed a little overwhelmed so I offered to help her deliver them."

"Oh? She was upset?" Charlotte locked her eyes to his.

"Not upset exactly, just distracted I guess. She had some of the boxes on different tables, but I helped her get it all straightened out. What was your name again? I can see if she was planning to give you a gift and let her know that she missed delivering yours." He pulled out his phone.

"Oh no, please don't. I'd be embarrassed. I'll just

ask her about it next time I see her. Thanks!" She waved to him and hurried off down the hall before he could ask her any more questions. Her heart pounded as she did the math. It was possible that Diana had slipped the few doors to Martin's place, killed him, and then set out to deliver gifts. It gave her a good alibi, were it not for Andy remembering the exact time they set out. She headed straight for the shop, eager to share the information with Ally. Diana was looking more and more suspicious, and from what Ally had told her Nina appeared to be her friend. If Ally was alone with a murderer because she had convinced her not to fire her, she would never forgive herself.

∼

*A*bout an hour before closing, Charlotte walked through the door.

"Mee-Maw, you're supposed to be relaxing." Ally raised an eyebrow.

"Not a chance. I'm going to help you get caught up. Plus, we need to talk." Her tone grew serious. "Alone." She cut a glance in Nina's direction.

"Nina, can you finish up the order in the back for me, please?" Ally asked.

"Sure." She glanced at Charlotte, spared her a smile, then headed into the back.

"What is it, Mee-Maw?" Ally leaned across the counter. "What did you find out?"

"I found out that Diana doesn't have an alibi for the time of the murder, and she had plenty of motive to kill Martin."

"And she and Nina are pretty good friends." Ally frowned. "But I can't see Diana doing this, can you? She seems so frail. What if Nina did it to protect her?"

"Shh." Charlotte looked towards the kitchen. "We still don't have any proof. Knowing who it likely is, isn't enough. We need to have a way to prove it."

"Maybe we do have a way." Ally's eyes widened as she looked over at her grandmother. "As Jeff said, if there was a camera up on any of these apartments then the person breaking in would have been caught. Our theory is that perhaps someone is breaking in to these apartments to find evidence of who the killer is, or the killer is breaking in to find something."

"Which still doesn't make complete sense to me." Charlotte sighed.

"No, it doesn't, but if that's two of our theories,

then maybe the person is still going to look for whatever they are looking for. We might find the killer or the robber, or both. If we can set up a hidden camera on one of the apartments that are left from the list, then we might just find our killer." Ally smiled.

"That's assuming that they haven't found what they are looking for. I mean, maybe the break-ins have stopped because they found what they were looking for." Charlotte gazed up at the ceiling for a moment. "But, if whatever it is hasn't been found yet, this is the perfect opportunity, you're right. Setting the trap might prove to be impossible, though. We don't know for certain whose apartments are being broken into. At first, we thought it was people in the class, but Jeff wasn't in the class."

"No, but you were." Ally sat forward in her chair. As her feet struck the floor she felt even more determined that she was on the right track. "Jeff is connected to you. Maybe, for some reason the person went to Jeff's house instead of yours. Did he mention receiving any kind of delivery?" She met her grandmother's eyes.

"A delivery?" Charlotte pursed her lips as she searched her memory. "Oh. Oh no!" Charlotte clasped her hand over her mouth for a moment, then slowly lowered it. "Oh, Ally."

"What is it, Mee-Maw?" She crossed the distance between them.

"It couldn't be."

"Just tell me," Ally insisted. "Whatever it is, I trust your instincts. You're not going to be able to ignore it."

"Jeff said that Diana stopped by his apartment with one of her giftboxes. It's the only gift he mentioned receiving. I know the evidence is stacking up against her, but it's just so hard for me to believe. Why would she hide something in a box of chocolates? Why would she deliver it to Jeff?"

"She didn't find it in his apartment, did she?" Ally narrowed her eyes.

"No, because he re-gifted it to someone else!"

"It actually makes sense. Think about it, Mee-Maw. All of the people that have been broken into were connected to the class in some way, and Diana was in that class as well. But she hasn't been broken into, has she?"

"No, but some of the other students haven't and neither have I..." Charlotte frowned.

"She didn't give you a gift. I mean I doubt that she would give your own chocolates back to you and she didn't give you a giftbox. Let's say that somehow evidence that she was the murderer is in one of those gifts. I have no idea why she would put it in there, but let's just say that it is. Of course, she's going to want to try to get it back. Most people wait until Christmas to open their gifts, so maybe she hoped she could get it back before anyone saw it."

"If that's the case, as terrible as it is, then she needs to be caught. She's already killed once, and who knows what she will do if she doesn't find what she is looking for. Maybe she will stop just breaking in and take it a step farther. Or what if someone catches her?" Charlotte squeezed Ally's hand. "We have to find out for sure as soon as we can. Especially if Nina is involved."

"I have an idea. Why don't we pick someone's apartment who is in the class, someone who has not been broken into, yet. Someone that received a gift. We can mention the name to Nina and maybe she will tell Diana. We'll say that they are excited to open their gift from her and can't wait until Christmas to do it. That will make her need to search the apartments urgent, if she put something in the gift. We can set up a camera outside of the apartment and even stake it out ourselves to see if she tries to break in."

"I don't know." Charlotte's heart pounded. "It makes me nervous to think of making someone vulnerable to a break-in, or even worse."

"If she shows up, we'll find a way to distract her, to stop her from going in at all. The person will never be at risk. In fact, I know the perfect person to set up." Ally's eyes shone with determination. "Beth."

"Beth?" Charlotte sat forward some. "Why Beth?"

"Because she's our other suspect. So, if Diana never shows up to break in, we'll still get a record of things Beth does during that time. Maybe she will do something to implicate herself." She shrugged. "It would be like killing two birds with one stone."

"Why would I ever want to kill a bird?" Charlotte raised an eyebrow.

"I love you, Mee-Maw." She hugged her. "You always make me smile."

"You too, my love. Now, if we're going to do this, we'd better get it done tonight. I know that Jeff was looking into cameras to purchase for his apartment, and for mine, so I'll check with him on what we might be able to get." She pursed her lips, then shook her head. "Such a shame that it's coming to this. But whoever did this probably thinks they got away with it, now that Trudy is in jail. We can't let that happen."

"I believe she's innocent, too, Mee-Maw, but the only way we're going to get her out is if we find out who really did it. I'll make the comment to Nina. You go check on things with Jeff, and we'll meet up near Beth's apartment after closing. Okay?"

"Yes, sounds good." As Charlotte headed out the door, she felt enlivened by the thought that they might catch the killer. The sensation was dampened by the possibility that it would turn out to be a friend.

CHAPTER 16

As Ally prepared to close the shop, she noticed that Nina was quiet.

"You know, I do hope that Diana brings me one of her boxes to put on display." Ally smiled as she closed out the register. "Everyone is saying how nice they are. Earlier today, Beth said she was going to open up her box tonight and eat up all of the chocolates. I'm sure they will taste so much sweeter because they came in such a beautifully designed box."

"That's nice of you to say, Ally." Nina smiled. "If I see Diana I'll be sure to tell her that you want one." She pulled out her phone as she headed out the door. "I'll be here first thing in the morning."

"That's all right, take tomorrow morning off. I don't want to wear you out." Ally grinned.

"Thanks!" She waved to Ally then stepped out the door, as she was typing. Ally couldn't help but wonder if she might be texting Diana to let her know about Beth's intentions. If that was the case then their plan had worked, but it also meant that Nina was involved which she didn't want to believe. As she finished up with the shop she received a text from Charlotte.

Jeff already had some cameras and we figured out a way to hide them. We're already set up near Beth's apartment. You should go home and rest, too many people here will draw attention.

Ally frowned and texted her back.

I don't want you there by yourself, Mee-Maw. I'll be there soon. I just want to feed Arnold and Peaches.

On the drive home, Ally's heart raced. This was it, they might find out the truth. She arrived at the cottage in a rush. As she hurried to feed Peaches and Arnold, she barely noticed how restless they were. On the way back out the door, she picked up Peaches for a quick kiss. The cat purred and rubbed her cheek against Ally's. Ally put Peaches on the floor. Peaches stared up at her. Then she began to pace back and forth across the floor in front of the door. It seemed as if she was trying to stop her from leaving.

"Peaches, honey, it's okay I promise." She crouched down and took a moment to pet the cat. Arnold wandered over to soak up some of her affection, too. "I'm sorry, guys, I've been so preoccupied, and I know that you must wonder what's going on. Hopefully, it will all be over tonight." She kissed them each on the top of the head, then stepped out of the cottage. On her way to Freely Lakes she remembered the way Arnold had snorted at the list she dropped on the floor, and Peaches' reaction to the picture of the Blue River Belles. Had they been trying to tell her something? She laughed as she realized how ridiculous that seemed.

As she parked, her cell phone rang. She saw that it was Luke, and decided to take it. She didn't think much would be happening yet on the stakeout.

"Hi sweetie."

"Hi love. How are you doing?"

"Okay, I guess." She sighed. "We think we might have a new suspect."

"Oh? Have you told the chief about it?"

"No, not yet. I think he has a problem with me for some reason."

"Oh yeah, that might be my fault."

"Huh? Why?"

"I had just been on a conference call with him

when we talked, and you made that comment about his hair. Somehow the calls were still connected."

"Are you serious?" She groaned. "Please tell me you're joking."

"Sorry, sweetheart, I wish I was. I think his ego took a hit."

"Luke!"

"Try not to worry about it, I'm sure he'll get over it. I'm still working on a ticket."

"Hopefully, you'll work something out."

She hung up the phone, mortified by Luke's revelation, and headed into Freely Lakes.

~

"Just go, Jeff. I can handle this." Charlotte frowned as she tried to guide him towards the elevator.

"If you're going to be here, I'm going to be here, too." He locked eyes with her and raised an eyebrow. "Any questions?"

She opened her mouth to let him know that she did have a few things to say about that, but before she could speak, there was a noise at the end of the hallway.

"Just come here." She huffed and pulled him

back behind a large plant. There was barely enough room for two. When she peered through the leaves she saw what the noise was caused by. A figure had come out of the stairwell. Whoever it was wanted to avoid the elevators. That was unusual at Freely Lakes, as the stairs were usually only used during emergencies and fire drills. As the figure approached, she was disappointed by the fact that she couldn't make out much about it. It could have been a woman, or a small-statured man. There was no indication of age. The person was dressed in dark clothing with a hood pulled down low to cover their features, and blended with the shadows at the edge of the hallway. When the person reached the door of Beth's apartment, Charlotte's heartbeat quickened. This was it, this was the moment when she would find out the truth.

"We should go now." Jeff started to step out from behind the plant, but Charlotte placed a hand on his arm to stop him.

"Not yet," she hissed. She wanted to see the person actually try to break into Beth's apartment. Otherwise they would still have no proof. She wasn't sure that the camera would take a clear enough picture, and with the disguise the person was wearing, there would be no way to prove who it was. Jeff nodded, and slid back against the wall. The figure glanced around. Were their voices heard?

Charlotte held her breath. If even a leaf on the plant fluttered, she was sure that they would be caught. A second later, the figure turned back to the door. Charlotte could hear the sound of the person's attempts to pry through the lock. She was about to nod to Jeff, when the door to the apartment flung open.

"What do you think you're doing?" Beth shouted at the person. She had her robe tied up tight around her, and a baseball bat in her hands. "Get out of here!" Beth swung the bat, but missed, as the person ducked. The person stumbled backward, and tripped over the carpet.

"Beth wait!" Charlotte jumped out from behind the tree just as Beth was about to swing the bat down against the criminal's head.

"Charlotte?" Beth dropped the bat in shock. Jeff followed right behind Charlotte. "Was it you?" Beth stared at them. "Are you the cause of all of this?"

"No! It was this person!" Charlotte leaned down and tugged the hood up off the face of the figure on the floor. Her eyes widened as it revealed Diana's face covered in tears.

"I'm so sorry, I'm so sorry." She held her hands up in the air. "I never meant to cause any trouble."

Charlotte crouched over her. "How could you do this, Diana? Why?" Up until the very last moment, she hoped that Diana would prove to be innocent. She was shocked to see her friend lying there.

"I'll call the police." Jeff pulled out his phone and began to dial.

"I'm not saying another word. Not another word!" She shook her head.

"Oh Diana." Charlotte sighed. "Martin might not have been the greatest man, but he didn't deserve to die."

"Mee-Maw!" Ally ran down the hall towards her. "What happened?"

Charlotte kept a close eye on the woman on the floor as she filled Ally in on what had happened. Beth paced back and forth, the bat still in her hand.

As police officers began to flood the hallway, Ally realized that it really was over. But just as she began to relax, she caught sight of another figure, one she recognized. Nina stood at the entrance of the stairs, then ducked back out of sight. Ally chased after her without a second of hesitation. She caught up with her at the lobby, just as the chief walked in. Ally grabbed her by the arm and held her tight.

"Nina! What are you doing here?"

"Ally? What's going on?" The chief crossed his arms as he looked between the two women.

"Chief, she was in the stairwell, I believe she was part of all of this."

"Not exactly." Nina gazed down at her feet. "I really wasn't, Ally." She met her eyes. "Diana came to me, she told me the truth about what she'd done, and begged me for help."

"So, you helped her break into the apartments?" Ally asked.

"I did but I didn't hurt Martin, I didn't!"

"Withholding information about a crime and covering up for it after makes you an accessory." The chief turned her around and began to cuff her.

"She had no one," Nina mumbled distractedly. "She was just so lonely. How could she ever survive in prison?"

"Did you call in the anonymous tips to the police with evidence to implicate Charlotte Sweet?" the chief asked.

"I'm sorry, Ally." Nina frowned as she was led away by an officer. "I knew Luke would have been able to get her out of it. Diana had no one."

"Terrible. How could you?" Ally shook her head and stared at her as she was led away to one of the police cars. She imagined that with Nina's testimony the police probably wouldn't even need a confession from Diana.

"Are you coming?" The chief held the elevator door open for Ally. Silently, she stepped inside. It was awkward to stand beside him, knowing that he was likely angry with her. She was certain that he would have a problem with the fact that they were involved. In her mind she ran through the speech that she was sure he would deliver.

"You never should have mounted a camera, you put Beth at risk, you should have left the police work to the police."

As he sauntered out of the elevator to join the others, she mentally prepared herself for what would come next. He assessed the scene, then spoke to Diana.

"Do you want to tell me what happened?"

One of the officers helped her to her feet.

"Nina, Nina will help me!" she gasped.

"Nina has already been arrested, Diana, and if you want to do anything to help her, you need to tell the truth." The chief fixed her with a steady gaze. "Why did you do it?"

"He was going to sell my apartment. My home, it was all I had. I tried to reason with him. I went over there with a gift for Trudy and Martin, but I really just wanted the excuse to beg him for my apartment. But he laughed at me, called me pathetic. I guess he was still angry from his fight with Victoria and Trudy. He shoved me and told me to get out of his apartment. I snapped, I grabbed the scissors from the counter. I just wanted him to stop shoving me!" She blinked back tears. "He was going to take everything from me!"

"And then what?" Ally stepped up beside her grandmother. "You left him there?"

"Yes, I went back to my place. I was in a panic, I didn't know what to do."

"Why did you break into all of the apartments?" Charlotte asked.

"When I got back to my place, I got changed and there was a knock on the door. I had no idea who it was. I didn't have any time to hide the scissors properly. So, I tucked it into one of the boxes of chocolates and put it aside to take care of later. When I opened the door I expected to find the police, but there was Andy. He was dropping off my paint brushes. He insisted that he help me deliver the boxes. I think he likes me, he was always trying to help me. I refused at first, but he insisted. I thought it might help me with my alibi if I was with someone around the time of the murder." She shook her head. "The box with the scissors was off to the side, but Andy must have mixed them up! I didn't even know it, until I got back and the box was gone."

"So you broke into the apartments to get the weapon back?" Ally asked.

"I did, Nina helped me. I knew it would only be a matter of time before someone found the scissors. But I couldn't find it. I took some random items to try to cover up what I was looking for." She wept as her body trembled. "I feel terrible. I just wanted to keep my home."

One of the officers led her away as she continued to cry. Ally slipped her hand into her grandmother's. The chief turned to face them.

"Although, I have to say that I'm impressed with the little scheme you came up with, and in the end it did work you never should have done it. You put everyone at risk." He scanned his gaze across Charlotte, Ally, and Jeff. "Unfortunately, there's that one thing that's still missing. It would really make our case against Diana much stronger."

"The murder weapon?"

"Yes." The chief nodded. "Without it, it will be hard to prove that Diana committed the crime."

"But isn't her presence here and what she has said the same as an admission of guilt?" Jeff crossed his arms as he looked at the chief. "Are you saying there's a chance she could get away with this?"

"It's okay, Jeff." Charlotte placed her hand on his arm.

"It's just that it would be easier to get a conviction with the murder weapon," the chief said.

"It has to turn up eventually, right?" Jeff asked.

"Yes, hopefully not on Christmas morning. That would be an awful surprise for someone." Charlotte's eyes widened.

"I'm sure we'll find it before then." The chief nodded to the three of them, then headed back over to Beth to speak to her.

Ally was relieved that the murder had been solved, but left unsettled by the missing weapon.

CHAPTER 17

The next day was Christmas Eve. Ally went into the shop for a few hours in the morning, then closed up, and headed back to the cottage to prepare a feast. While she prepared some of the food, she kept her phone close. Peaches wound around her legs and wouldn't leave her side. She smiled as she reached down to pet her. She tried to relax and take her mind off the events of the last few days by painting chocolate inside some cupcake liners to make chocolate cups. Even though she worked with chocolate for most of the day she still loved it and it helped her to relax. Once the chocolate cups were in the refrigerator setting, she began making the brandy chocolate mousse to go inside them. Charlotte had mentioned that Jeff loved brandy and she knew that Luke did, too. She licked the spoon and sighed with contentment. Rich, yet delicious. She wished that Luke was there to try some. She put the spoon in the sink and the mousse in the refrigerator.

Now that some of the prep work was done, she settled on the couch. She couldn't stop thinking about whether Luke would make it so she tried to distract herself by reading a magazine. Instead, she ended up staring at her phone. She willed it to ring. She had no idea if Luke's plane had taken off, or if it would land any time soon. She hadn't heard from him since that morning when he told her he was trying to find his way home. As much as she wanted to see him, she was more concerned about his safety. She hoped that if the weather wasn't good, the plane didn't take off.

As the turkey cooked in the oven the scent of it filled the air. Soon, her grandmother and Jeff would arrive for dinner, and whether Luke made it or not, they would celebrate. Martin's murder was solved, and Blue River could be considered safe again. As upsetting as the entire event was, Christmas would still lift spirits, and by the time the New Year came around, it would be just a memory.

Peaches hopped up onto the coffee table, and knocked her phone to the floor.

"Peaches!" Ally sighed, then laughed as the cat made the next leap into her lap. "Yes, I know. I'm sitting around when there's so much to do." She stood up and began to set the table. As she did, she turned the television on to hear the weather.

"It may be a white Christmas after all. The band that looked like it would pass us by, has changed direction. It's still a little uncertain about whether it will be too warm, but keep your eyes open for the possibility."

"Hmm, what do you think, Arnold? Will it be a white Christmas?"

The pig lifted his head from his cozy bed and snorted. Then he rested his head once more.

"Ah yes, you don't care do you?" She smiled as she gazed out through the kitchen window. The sun had begun to set, and the sky was thick with heavy clouds. It looked like snow. Maybe that would bring a little of the magic back into the holiday for everyone. It couldn't deter a plane from landing, perhaps just lace the trees with white, but it might be enough to cheer up the town. She hummed to herself as she stirred the pots on the stove. When there was a light knock on the door she turned with a smile to greet her grandmother.

"Ally, it smells wonderful in here!" She grinned.

"What can I help with?" She pulled her granddaughter into a tight hug.

"Everything is cooking, now we just need to light up the tree." She tipped her head towards the dark pine tree in the corner. They usually organized it earlier, but because they had been so busy with everything it had been left till the last minute.

"Allow me." Charlotte's smile spread wide as she walked over to the tree. Jeff paused beside Ally.

"She's so happy to spend this time with you, Ally."

"So am I." Ally clapped as the tree lit up. It reminded her of the many Christmases she'd spent in her grandmother's cottage. No matter where she and her grandmother lived, they always spent Christmas together.

"It's beautiful." Jeff nodded, as a wistful smile crept across his lips. It faded after a moment, and he looked between the two women. "I have to tell you something."

"What is it?" Charlotte squeezed his hand. She could see the change in his expression. "I'm sure whatever it is can't be that bad."

"But it is." He shook his head. "It's terrible."

"Just tell me, Jeff." Her heart dropped as she recalled Victoria's proclamation that Jeff had been spending a lot of time with Trudy. Was he going to tell her that now that Trudy was cleared of any wrongdoing, he'd decided he'd rather be with her? It surprised her that the possibility bothered her so much. She really had grown very fond of Jeff.

"I found the murder weapon." He took her other hand in his, and held them both.

"The scissors?" Charlotte blinked.

"That's great news!" Ally smiled

"It was in my box of chocolates that I gave to Michael," Jeff said. "If I had only opened it, I might have solved this entire crime the day it happened."

"Jeff, it's not your fault. You couldn't have known. At least, we have the murder weapon now. That will help bring Diana to justice. As much as I hate to say it, as I once believed that Diana was my friend, she deserves to face the consequences for her actions. She had other options." Charlotte frowned. "Still, I can't imagine what it would be like to feel alone and desperate to try and keep your home. I am so lucky to have Ally, and you." She met his eyes. "Don't ever think that I feel differently."

"It's all right, Charlotte." He wrapped his arms around her and pressed his lips against her forehead in a light kiss. "I know how much you care."

"Oh my, you two are so sweet I might have to

reduce some of the sugar in these desserts." Ally grinned as she spooned the mousse into the chocolate cups.

"Oh hush, I've witnessed a lot of gushy mushy moments between you and Luke." Charlotte grinned, but her amusement faded almost instantly. "Oh, Ally I'm sorry. You must miss him."

"It's okay, Mee-Maw." She laughed. "You're right, besides I'll see him soon enough." She glanced through the kitchen window. "It really does look like it might snow. I'd better take Arnold for a walk now, or he might not be brave enough to traipse through the white stuff."

"Okay, I'll keep an eye on things in here." Charlotte walked over to the stove. Ally smiled to herself as she was sure her grandmother was dying to check on things from the moment she walked in. As she stepped outside with Arnold on his leash, the chill in the air made her shiver. Her breath froze for a moment as she exhaled. She laughed to herself. Yes, it finally felt like Christmas. Not only because of the scent of snow in the air, but because of the pressure that had been lifted off her shoulders. The murder had been solved, the right people were behind bars, and now, everyone could relax and celebrate the holidays. Arnold snorted and tugged her along. She tried to hold him back.

"Steady, Arnold."

Arnold snorted again and strained against his harness. She rolled her eyes as the pig tugged her down the driveway. As soon as he reached the end of it he began to squeal and dance back and forth. "What in the world has gotten into you, Arnold? Did you get a sip of eggnog?"

"I think he's happy to see me." The voice drifted to her from the sidewalk that met the driveway.

"Luke!" She gasped and turned to face him. "You're here!"

"I'm here!" He laughed as a taxi pulled away from the sidewalk. He started to speak again, but his breath was stolen by the crush of Ally's arms as she hugged him.

"I didn't think you were going to make it!" She gazed into his eyes, as Arnold continued to snort and squeal beside them.

"I didn't think I was either. It took a good amount of determination and an incredible amount of luck. I caught the first taxi I saw." He stole a kiss, then met her eyes. "I just didn't want to miss this moment with you, Ally."

"I would have picked you up if you called. I

would have been waiting for you there at the airport." She kissed him in return.

"I know you would have, that's why I didn't tell you. I wasn't sure if things might fall through. But here I am." He smiled as a snowflake drifted down between them.

"Here you are." She gazed at him, her heart so warm that she didn't notice the icy breeze that sent several more snowflakes down from the sky. "I love you, Luke."

"I love you, too." He kissed her again.

Despite the frigid temperatures, neither seemed to notice, and the pig that lingered at their feet, caught a snowflake on the tip of his nose.

The End

CHOCOLATE BRANDY MOUSSE CUPS

Ingredients:

Chocolate Brandy Mousse:

10 ounces bitter-sweet chocolate

3 large egg whites

2 tablespoons superfine sugar

1 1/2 cups whipping cream

1-2 tablespoons brandy (optional)

Chocolate cups:

8 ounces semi-sweet chocolate

Decorations:

6 strawberries or raspberries to decorate
Confectioners' sugar for decorating (optional)

Preparation:

Makes 6 brandy mousse filled chocolate cups.

Place 6 cupcake liners on a baking sheet lined with parchment paper.

For the brandy mousse chop the chocolate into pieces and gently melt in a double boiler. Once melted set aside to cool slightly.

In a bowl whip the egg whites until slightly cloudy then add the superfine sugar gradually. Beat until stiff peaks form.

In another bowl whip the cream until soft peaks form.

Fold the whipped egg whites into the chocolate mixture.

Fold the cream into the chocolate egg white mixture.

Add the brandy and mix gently until well-combined.

Place in the refrigerator for about 15 minutes to set slightly.

For the chocolate cups gently melt the chocolate preferably in a double boiler.

With a spoon divide the melted chocolate between the cupcake liners and using a pastry brush paint the bottom and sides of each liner until the inside is completely coated.

Place on the baking sheet lined with parchment paper.

Refrigerate for about 15 minutes until set.

Once set gently peel the paper cups from the chocolate.

Fill each chocolate cup with the slightly set chocolate brandy mousse.

Place in the refrigerator for one to two hours to set further.

Place a strawberry or raspberry on the top of each cup before serving.

Sprinkle the top of each chocolate cup with a bit of confectioners' sugar to look like snow.

Enjoy!

CHOCOLATE CHRISTMAS TREE COOKIES

Ingredients:

3/4 cup cold butter

2/3 cup granulated sugar

1 egg

1 teaspoon vanilla extract

1/2 cup unsweetened cocoa powder

1 3/4 cups all-purpose flour

1 teaspoon baking powder

Decorations:

7 ounces bitter-sweet chocolate

4 ounces white chocolate

Preparation:

Line a baking sheet with parchment paper.

Cube the butter and place in a bowl with the sugar. Mix with a handheld or stand mixer until light and fluffy.

Add the egg and vanilla extract and mix until well-combined.

Sift the cocoa powder, flour and baking powder together.

Gradually add the flour and cocoa mixture a spoonful at a time to the butter sugar mixture.

Mix until combined.

On a floured surface roll the dough to about a 1/4 inch thick.

Wrap the dough in cling film and place in the refrigerator for approximately an hour.

Preheat the oven to 375 degrees Fahrenheit.

Remove the cooled dough from the refrigerator and using Christmas tree cookie cutters cut out the trees.

Place the cookies on the baking sheet lined with parchment paper.

Place in the oven for 7-10 minutes. They are ready when the sides are firm to the touch and the middle is still a bit soft. They will firm up more while they are cooling.

For the decorations gently melt the bitter-sweet chocolate, preferably in a double boiler. Leave it aside to cool slightly.

Dip the cooled cookies into the melted bitter-sweet chocolate and then grate white chocolate over the top to look like snow.

Leave aside to set.

Enjoy!

ALSO BY CINDY BELL

DUNE HOUSE COZY MYSTERIES

Seaside Secrets

Boats and Bad Guys

Treasured History

Hidden Hideaways

Dodgy Dealings

Suspects and Surprises

Ruffled Feathers

A Fishy Discovery

Danger in the Depths

Celebrities and Chaos

Pups, Pilots and Peril

BEKKI THE BEAUTICIAN COZY MYSTERIES

Hairspray and Homicide

A Dyed Blonde and a Dead Body

Mascara and Murder

SAGE GARDENS COZY MYSTERIES

Snow Can Be Deadly

Tea Can Be Deadly

A MACARON PATISSERIE COZY MYSTERY SERIES

Sifting for Suspects

Recipes and Revenge

Mansions, Macarons and Murder

NUTS ABOUT NUTS COZY MYSTERIES

A Tough Case to Crack

A Seed of Doubt

HEAVENLY HIGHLAND INN COZY MYSTERIES

Murdering the Roses

Dead in the Daisies

Killing the Carnations

Drowning the Daffodils

Suffocating the Sunflowers

Books, Bullets and Blooms

A Deadly Serious Gardening Contest

A Bridal Bouquet and a Body

Digging for Dirt

CHOCOLATE CENTERED COZY MYSTERIES

The Sweet Smell of Murder

A Deadly Delicious Delivery

A Bitter Sweet Murder

A Treacherous Tasty Trail

Luscious Pastry at a Lethal Party

Trouble and Treats

Fudge Films and Felonies

Custom-Made Murder

Skydiving, Soufflés and Sabotage

WENDY THE WEDDING PLANNER COZY MYSTERIES

Matrimony, Money and Murder

Chefs, Ceremonies and Crimes

Knives and Nuptials

Mice, Marriage and Murder

Cindy Bell is the author of the cozy mystery series Donut Truck, Dune House, Sage Gardens, Chocolate Centered, Macaron Patisserie, Nuts about Nuts, Bekki the Beautician, Heavenly Highland Inn and Wendy the Wedding Planner.

Cindy has always loved reading, but it is only recently that she has discovered her passion for writing romantic cozy mysteries. She loves walking along the beach thinking of the next adventure her characters can embark on.

You can sign up for her newsletter so you are notified of her latest releases at http://www.cindybellbooks.com.

Made in the USA
Columbia, SC
14 October 2023